PROMISES

LORI BEASLEY BRADLEY

Published 2021 by Next Chapter

Edited by Emily Fuggetta

Cover art by CoverMint

Back cover texture by David M. Schrader, used under license from Shutterstock.com

Mass Market Paperback Edition

❦ 1 ❦

Ivy Chandler leaned on the railing of the resort hotel's balcony, staring out at the expansive desert cast in shades of red and gold in the setting sun. A warm, damp breeze ruffled her hair, and lightning flashed jagged in the darkening sky.

Ivy had grown up in the Midwest where humidity levels in August reached into the upper ninety-percent range, and she rolled her eyes every time she heard the Arizona locals whine about twenty-five percent. If luck held, the lightening meant a cooling summer storm.

Her hair lifted from her neck, and she felt his hot breath on her shoulder as he nuzzled her. Carl's body, damp and cool from the shower, rubbed against hers as he snaked his arms around and into her loose robe to find her breasts. He pinched her nipples, and she moaned as they firmed into throbbing buttons between his fingers. Ivy leaned back into his sturdy body.

"You're a devil," she sighed, enjoying the way her body reacted to his touch. Carl pinched harder, and her clit began to throb along with her nipples. Ivy reached behind her and stroked Carl's erection as it oozed a bit onto the back of her thigh. She shivered with every pinch and twist he gave her.

"Come on, baby." He pulled Ivy closer, and his erection nudged her behind. "Let's go to bed. Close those patio doors on your way in, or the room will be full of sand." Carl Anderson tugged her silky robe from her shoulders and let it slide to the floor of the concrete patio.

Ivy turned and watched him drag it into the plush room. He pulled back the ornate spread to reveal white cotton sheets. "Come on, baby." Carl sprawled across the bed and stroked his erection for her to see. "He needs you, baby. He needs you bad."

Ivy followed Carl in and shut the multi-paned French doors. She made her way to the bed and joined him. Ivy bent and lowered her mouth onto his waiting erection.

Carl's body tensed with the touch of her soft lips. She used her tongue to remove the pre-cum from the head and gave it a little tickle on that spot where the head met the shaft. Ivy felt him shiver with pleasure as she tightened her mouth around his stiff cock. Carl moaned with pleasure and threaded his fingers through her hair, pushing her head further down on his erection. Ivy stroked his cock with her mouth for a few minutes before pulling back.

"Don't stop now, baby," he pleaded. "I need it. I need it now."

"Sweetie, you have sex on the brain." She fell back and shivered as his strong hand trailed down her belly to rest in the mound of silky hair between her thighs. His fingers massaged her clit, sending thrills through her groin and her breasts as well.

"Oh, Carl," Ivy sighed, "don't stop. Make me cum with your finger first." She spread her legs wider and rubbed his erection with her smooth, firm thigh.

"I might be old, baby, but I'm not dead yet. I have needs." He bent and took a nipple into his mouth and sucked hard, nipping it playfully with his even, white teeth.

Ivy ran her hand through his thick, white hair and moaned, "Harder." She reached down and began massaging his throbbing erection. She teased the head with her fingertips before grasping his hard cock fully in her hand and stroking it gently, tightening and loosening her hold as he pumped into her tanned fist.

"You have magic fingers, baby." He rolled atop her and looked down into her blue eyes with his own. She continued stroking him, and his eyes rolled up into his head. "Keep that up, and I'm gonna have to give it to you good." Ivy stroked him and gave his hanging balls a soft squeeze.

"You always give it to me good, sweetie." She clutched his erection and pulled on it.

Carl continued to finger her hot wetness and massage her throbbing clit until Ivy writhed and moaned beneath him with pleasure upon the expensive sheets.

"I want you in me now, sweetie," she said, panting. "You're driving me crazy. I can't wait." Ivy arched into his probing fingers with enthusiasm. Carl removed his fingers from her crevasse and braced his arms on the pillow beside her head, positioning himself above her body as he eased himself into her. Ivy moaned, wrapped her arms around his neck, and pulled his face down to her own. Their lips met, and his tongue pushed past her teeth to find hers. She luxuriated in the hot, salty taste of him.

Ivy met his pounding thrusts with vigor until the throbbing between her thighs exploded in exquisite waves of pleasure.

"Oh, my God, I'm cumming, Carl, I'm cumming." Her pulsing orgasm triggered his, and Carl groaned and shivered atop her. His sweat dripped onto her face before he rolled his spent body off hers, panting.

"Oh, baby, you milk me nice," he said, breathless beside her.

Ivy ran her fingers through her sweat-damp brunette hair, kept dark with bottles of Miss Clairol regularly now that she had reached her mid-fifties.

"How long are we going to keep this up, Carl?" Ivy asked, looking up at the paddles of the ceiling fan as they turned slowly above them. "Neither of us is getting any younger. How long are we going to keep sneaking around like a couple of kids?" Ivy broached the subject with caution.

The two had been seeing one another for nearly a year, and Ivy had hoped the relationship would advance past the bedroom, but it hadn't. She turned her head on the soft pillow to see him staring up at the ceiling blankly.

Maybe I gave in too easy. He doesn't respect me. I should have played at being one of those born-again virgins he's always complaining about. He really wants a woman he could bring home to his momma, not a play toy. I'm good enough for weekdays when he's not traveling, but not good enough to take on his damned trips to meet his family and friends.

Carl propped himself up on his elbow and looked down at her with a spark of irritation in his clear, blue eyes. "Baby, we've been over this before. I travel too much for any more of a relationship than this."

He slapped her playfully on her bare hip. "You know you love this. You get to stay in a nice place for a few days and get the best sex you've had in your life." He chuckled and fell back onto his pillows. "Do you want to go out, or should we order room service?"

Ivy did not look at him but sat up and swung her long legs off the bed. "Suit yourself." She snatched two tissues from the box by the bed and wiped him from between her thighs before it could run down her legs. "I'm gonna take a hot shower."

"Room service it is," he said with a snort and picked up the phone. Ivy listened as he ordered T-bones rare, potatoes loaded, and salads with Thousand Island. No desserts. "Are you going to be mad at me all during dinner?" he asked as he rinsed his limp cock at the sink while she stepped into the shower.

"I'm not mad, Carl; just disappointed." Ivy stood under the hot water, letting the spray wash away her frustrated tears.

Ivy had fallen for the man after their first meeting for coffee and rolls at a Starbucks nearly a year before. They'd connected over mutual interests through a dating site, e-mailed for a few days, and then exchanged numbers and began texting and talking regularly. They both had Midwestern upbringings, college educations, marriages, divorces, and grown children. It had seemed to Ivy that they'd clicked.

After coffee, they'd ended up back at Ivy's apartment for a long afternoon of bedroom Olympics. For two people their ages, they had managed to sweat up the sheets and had 1enjoyed positions neither had attempted in years. The sex had been outstanding, and the conversations before and after even better.

Confident she'd found *the one*, Ivy had deleted her profile from the dating site and stopped speaking with other men she'd connected with there.

Ivy, an aspiring author, had self-published a couple of novels and continued to pursue the craft, even in these later years of her life. She enjoyed discussing her work with Carl, who encouraged her to follow her dream by pursuing publishing contracts and securing an agent.

While their meetings had continued in much the same way, a coffee or lunch followed by sex at her apartment, any time Ivy brought up taking their relationship to a more committed level, Carl brushed her off with excuses of needing to travel for his many real estate investment businesses and family trips. After a year, Ivy had yet to meet any of his family, and he'd turned down numerous invitations to meet hers.

Why am I wasting my time on this man? He's only in this for the sex. My God, I thought I'd gotten past this sort of shit after high school.

Ivy blew her nose into the washcloth, rinsed it, turned off the shower, and stepped out onto the bathmat. She yanked the thick Egyptian-cotton towel from the rack. Ivy wrapped her hair in the heavy towel and reached for another for her dripping body. She sat on the toilet to dry her long legs and inspected them. They didn't look as though they needed a shave yet, and she sighed to herself. She might be an older woman now, but she did her best to keep herself up.

Ivy didn't intend to be a woman like her mother, who'd turned sixty, gotten divorced, and stopped living or taking care of her physical appearance. Ivy's mother had died alone at sixty-five, and she didn't want to be the same.

Depression ran in her family, but Ivy did not intend to fall victim to it like other females in her mother's line. Two aunts had committed suicide, and her mother may have as well, though the doctors had assured Ivy and her sister, Carrie, it had been from complications after minor surgery.

The aroma of char-grilled beef met Ivy as she walked out of the bathroom. The little table beside the patio doors held the food and a bottle of her favorite sweet red wine. Carl attended to every tiny detail, and that endeared him to her. He remembered all her pleasures, including the wine she preferred with her steak.

Carl pulled out her chair. "Here you are, Madam. Your feast awaits you, as do I." He lifted the metal lid from her plate to reveal a juicy, rare T-bone with all the trimmings, including plump, yeasty rolls. Carl poured her wine and set the delicate long-stemmed glass beside one of iced water with a thin slice of lemon floating amongst the cubes.

Ivy inhaled the aroma of the food and realized how hungry she actually was. They'd eaten breakfast together in the hotel's dining room but skipped lunch to take a horseback ride through the juniper-strewn high-desert mountains above the resort.

Ivy loved horses but hadn't ridden since her childhood on the farm. Carl, a dedicated horseman, had criticized her for her inexperience and laughed maniacally when the stupid beast had thrown her in some loose scree on the side of the mountain. Fortunately, nothing but her ego had suffered more than a bruise, much to her relief. She couldn't afford a trip to the hospital with a broken bone.

Ivy took a long drink of the sweet wine then followed it with a longer one of the cold water.

"This looks lovely." Ivy picked up her fork and knife and began cutting to separate the meat from the long bone of the sumptuous steak. She set the bone aside and cut the meat into bite-sized pieces before sprinkling her potato with salt and pepper and dumping on the butter and sour cream.

She saw Carl watching her mash up the combination inside the brown shell of the potato skin. She wondered if he thought her a backward hick, treating her food the way she did.

Ivy didn't have the experience of sophisticated dining like he did and feared he looked down on her because of it. She could hold her own at a cocktail party, but she might embarrass him at a fancy dinner party. On the farm, a fork was a fork, and you used the same one for every course.

"Maybe I should have ordered you mashed potatoes," Carl chuckled. He sliced his salted and peppered potato, dipped it into his little cup of butter and then his sour cream before putting it into his mouth.

He cut the steak before each bite rather than all at once like her. Ivy preferred to eat her food in peace rather than working at it during her meal. Again, she suspected she shamed Carl with her gauche country eating habits.

I'm just not sophisticated enough for him. I'll never fit in with his country club crowd. I'm good enough for his bed. No, not even his *bed. He's never taken me to his home. He's been to my little apartment dozens of times, but I've never seen his.*

At least he takes me to nice hotels and not pay-by-the-hour dumps. I'll never admit to him that I've ever visited one of those. I'm just not good enough. He's never going to let me into his life any more than this. I should make my peace with that.

Tears stung Ivy's eyes again, but she batted them back and took another sip of wine. "The wine is perfect."

"Not the vintage I wanted, but a close second." He, too, took a drink, wiping his mouth with the white linen napkin afterward. "How is your steak? Rare enough?"

Ivy forked up one of the bloody pink cubes of beef and popped it into her mouth, savoring the succulent, warm juice flooding across her tongue. She chewed and swallowed.

"Delicious. Just the way I like it; only just a little past moo." Ivy liked her steaks very rare but well charred on the outside.

Her father had taught her how to cook steak on his old charcoal grill and insisted the flavor was in the red juices seared in by the flash charring over the hot coals. Ivy had agreed with her father on very few things, but his view on the grilling of steaks was one of them.

Her mother, on the other hand, had insisted on grilling her steaks to the consistency of shoe leather, rendering it inedible in Ivy's opinion. Carl liked his medium-rare with only the slightest pink juice running from them, and Ivy thought that blasphemous.

"Are you still upset with me?" He asked as he put a bite of spinach salad into his mouth.

"I'm not upset with you. I'm upset with this situation. You knew from the beginning I was looking for a committed relationship and not just a friends-with-benefits thing." Ivy was losing her appetite but refused to let the excellent meal go to waste. On her fixed income, steak dinners were few and far between.

"I'm committed to being friends with all the benefits for both of us." He picked up one of the dinner rolls and threw it at her.

With quick reflexes, Ivy caught the roll before it hit her in the face. "Just a whore for steak dinners and nice hotel rooms, am I?" Ivy snorted dryly.

"Don't forget the horseback rides," he said with a mischievous smile.

"Oh, yeah. Did you see the bruise on my ass?"

He lifted his wine glass in mock salute. "And a very lovely bruise it is."

"I didn't think I fell that hard, but it's certainly a doozy of a bruise."

"No grass up there to cushion the fall," he said thoughtfully as he buttered a roll for himself. "I think you went down on the solid rock. I'm surprised you didn't break something." He bit into the hot roll and chewed. "Maybe we should get you some restraints for the next time." Carl chuckled with his mouth full of the bread.

"I just bruise easily. I always have," Ivy said with a sneer.

"I remember the first time we did it from behind." He chuckled lasciviously. "You had my fingerprints bruised into your ass cheeks for a week."

She had to smile at the memory. "I know. I thought my sister was gonna have a cow when she saw them."

"Your sister sounds like a sour old prude. Has she ever enjoyed sex?" Carl took his final bite of potato, followed by a bite of steak.

"Says she has," Ivy sighed. "She just worries about me too much. She's afraid I'm going to get hurt."

"Are you?"

"Am I what?" Ivy finished her wine.

"Getting hurt?"

"Not physically," Ivy sighed and wiped her mouth. "Emotionally a little."

"I've been honest with you, Ivy. I'm too busy for more than what we have right here." He motioned around the charming Western-style room accented by its red-shaded hurricane lamps with clear dangling crystals of the nineteenth-century design. "If this isn't enough for you, then maybe we should rethink it. I've never made you any promises. Have I?"

"No, and I've been rethinking it, Carl, and rethinking again. I want more, but I want this, too." She let him refill her wine glass. "I love you, Carl, and you know it. I know I'm not the kind of woman you really want, but I'm here any time you want me. Maybe that's wrong, but it's what it is."

"Baby, I don't want to hurt you, and I want to be fair, but I'm in no position to take up a relationship of the sort you want right now. I need the sexual release, and you are a very sexy woman, but I have too many responsibilities right now to take on another."

"I know, sweetie. Let's just forget I brought it up and enjoy our evening." Ivy blinked back tears again and drank more wine. Wine always seemed to help her get over her disappointments where Carl was concerned. "I promise I won't bring it up again."

2

Two weeks after their return from the Apache Mountain Resort, Ivy stood in the small galley kitchen of her apartment, mixing some slaw to go with her pulled pork dinner.

Carl would be joining her soon, and she wanted to have everything ready when he arrived. Ivy dumped fries from the basket of the deep fryer on the counter.

This would be his last visit before going out of town again, and Ivy wanted everything to be perfect. They hadn't spoken much since their return from that trip, and it had worried her some. Then he'd messaged her on the computer, and she'd invited him for dinner. It had relieved Ivy when he'd happily accepted her invitation.

He's probably just horny. He needs to empty his cock before going out on the road again.

Her yellow tabby, Cheshire, twined between her feet, begging for dropped tidbits.

"Get out of here, you mooch. This is slaw, and you don't like it." The cat gave her a surly yowl but sauntered into the living room to take up his place on the couch. "There'll be pork later," Ivy assured him.

The doorbell rang, and Cheshire leaped from the couch and ran for the bedroom. "What a brave kitty you are," she said, chastising the cat. "I'm getting a dog." Ivy wiped her hands on a dishtowel and walked to the door.

"Hi, sweetie," she greeted Carl with a deep kiss.

"Smells good in here, baby. What you cookin'?" He handed her a paper sack from The Wine Seller. She opened it and brought out a bottle of Riesling.

"Pulled pork and slaw," Ivy told him, "and blackberry cobbler with ice cream for dessert."

"You know what I like, baby, but I was hoping for a little more for dessert." He slapped her behind. "How's the bruise?"

"All better. It's just a big tender yellow spot now."

Carl squeezed her behind. "I'll kiss it and make it all better after dinner."

"I'm sure you will," she laughed. "When are you leaving and where to this time?"

"In the morning around five. Have to be in Tulsa day after for a real estate conference."

"Cutting it close, aren't you? You should have gone today."

"Then I would have missed this fine dinner and the even finer dessert." He pinched her breast.

"Are you buying, selling, speaking, or all of it?" she asked as she put white china plates on the round oak table.

"I'm speaking on the importance of studying comps in the market and looking at a few places around the campus for rental properties." Carl sat in one of the sturdy oak chairs. "I was wondering if you'd like to join me on this trip."

Ivy looked at him in open-mouthed amazement. He'd never invited her to join him on one of his trips before, though she'd brought it up several times in the past, pointing out that she had no constraints on her time and was free to travel. He'd always brushed her off with excuses of this meeting or that.

This is a damned trick. He's springing it on me last-minute like this, thinking I'll say no because of Cheshire. Then I can't say he's never asked me to go with him.

"I'd love to, Carl." She watched his face for surprise. "I'll have to pack a bag real quick and call my sister about coming over to feed and water Cheshire, but I'd love to." She carried the bowl from the crockpot with the pork to the table and returned to the kitchen for the slaw and the buns. "Do you want to pick me up here in the morning or spend the night?"

"I thought I'd take you home with me tonight and leave from there in the morning." He poured the sweet white wine into glasses from the cabinet by the table and handed her one. "I know it's last-minute, but I really wanted to spend some time with you, Ivy, and I'm going to be coming right back here after the conference. Most of my trips are usually far longer," he said, sipping the wine, "so I thought this would finally be a good opportunity to see how we traveled together."

"Sounds good to me. I can throw a bag together after dinner. How long will we be gone?"

"Not more than a week. There will be one semi-formal cocktail thing, but business casual for the most part. Are you alright for that?" He fixed himself a sandwich and forked up some fries from the bowl. "This looks and smells great, baby. I know it's going to taste great too. So do you have the wardrobe for a week of boring conferences and boring cocktail parties?"

"I'm fine so long as there's an iron in the room so I can press the wrinkles from my clothes," Ivy said, giddy with anticipation. Mentally she went through her closet. A couple of skirts, jackets, slacks, and tanks should get her by for a week just fine.

Ivy had purchased most of her wardrobe so it could be combined to make up multiple outfits that would pass for business casual. Her black velvet dress would work for a cocktail party, and her black flats would do with it all. Jeans for travel, her swimsuit, and a long sleep shirt should round things out. By the time they'd finished their meal, Ivy had her mental packing completed.

"We'll be staying at the Clarion," Carl said, and Ivy thought he was trying to impress her with the fancy accommodations. "I'm sure there will be an iron available, or you can use the valet services." Carl began picking up the dishes and carrying them into the tiny but neat and tidy kitchen. "What do you want me to do with the leftovers?"

"There are containers with lids in the cabinet over the stove. Put the pork in one and throw it in the freezer along with the fries. The little bit of slaw can go down the disposal. If all the pork doesn't fit in the container, put some of it down for Cheshire. He loves pulled pork."

Ivy called her sister on her way into her bedroom and made arrangements for Carrie to check on the cat every few days, refill his food and water dishes, and clean out his litter box. Cheshire tended to be picky about his box and would throw a yowling fit if he thought it needed to be cleaned.

Luckily cats are solitary creatures that can amuse themselves and use a litter box. In her bedroom, Ivy pulled out the suitcase she'd just emptied from her trip to the resort and packed it with all the items she'd made a mental note of during dinner.

Ivy didn't think she'd ever packed as quickly in

her life. Luckily most of the toiletries were still in her overnight bag, and all she had to replace were her toothbrush, toothpaste, deodorant, and weekly med case. She made sure that was topped off and threw in the full bottles of her most essential.

The only meds I needed to worry about when I was younger were aspirin and birth control. Now there are blood pressure, cholesterol, and bullshit aches and pains. Getting old is a bitch. I'd better not forget my damned phone charger, either. What did the world do before cell phones? We had quiet time in the car, that's what. The only time we had to be worried about being bothered by pesky relatives or salesmen was at home. Now the cell phone has left us open to being pestered in our quietest moments. It is nice to have in case of a flat, though.

Ivy came from the bedroom, laden with her bags, and dropped them by the door. "Are you ready for some cobbler and ice cream?"

"Sounds good to me, baby. Did you get everything? Are you taking your laptop?"

"It's in my bag along with the cords, my phone charger, and my meds. I think I have it all."

"Did you bring your swimsuit? They have a nice indoor pool and a hot tub at the Clarion."

"Got it." Ivy dipped two heaping scoops of vanilla ice cream onto the warm blackberry cobbler and carried the bowls to the table. "I'll have another glass of wine with this. *I'm* not driving. Do you want coffee?"

"No, the ice cream is good enough. You're a great cook, baby."

"Just simple country fare, nothing special."

"It's special to me because I didn't have to cook it, and I'm not eating it in some lonesome restaurant." He dug into his dish with pleasure. "So good."

After cleaning up the dessert dishes and popping

the cobbler into the freezer, they carried Ivy's bags to Carl's Lexus and drove to his condo in Paradise Valley. Ivy was impressed, but she did her best not to let it show.

His luxury automobile made her nearly twenty-year-old sedan look like a piece of crap, and his condo made her efficiency apartment built sometime in the early eighties look like a slum.

I know he thinks I'm after him for his money. He has to believe that. Why wouldn't he? I'm poor and on a meager fixed income. He's a retired doctor and a successful real estate investor. What do I have to offer him besides what's between my legs and an adventurous imagination? I know he could do better than me in his own social circles. Maybe high-class women don't give it up as easily as classless, poor country trash like me. But I'm not classless.

I did the whole big money, high dollar country club thing back years ago when I was in retail. I went to those parties with lines of coke on the glass-topped coffee tables and Gull-wings and Porsches in the driveways. Been there, done that, remember the hangovers. It was fun at the moment, but those people were fake and stupid. They had their big houses and fancy cars but needed drugs and counterfeit friends to prop them up and make them feel important. I went to those parties in clothes from the Dress Barn, but I looked as good as they did, and I could carry on conversations with any of them. Screw this. I'm just as good as he is, and if he can't see that it's his loss, not mine.

"What's the matter, baby?" Carl asked when she didn't open her door after they'd parked in the garage. "Do you need both bags?"

"No, just the small one if these clothes are alright to travel in tomorrow." She looked down at her simple denim leggings and cotton tank top.

"You should wear what you feel comfortable in. You look great to me, baby."

Carl got out and walked around to open the door for her. Ivy appreciated that he still practiced these small civilities. Some women claimed real gentlemen didn't exist anymore, but Dr. Carl Anderson was a real gentleman who still opened doors and held a chair for a woman. Ivy never found it sexist or demeaning. She appreciated it. Maybe she *was* just an old-fashioned hick after all.

Ivy walked into an immaculate kitchen with stainless-steel appliances, granite countertops, and Italian marble floors. A black iron pot rack hung over a center island full of bright stainless-steel pots and pans. The glass lids sat atop the rack. Red and white gingham curtains hung at the windows, giving the room a distinctly country appeal. It would be a joy to cook in a kitchen like this.

Carl led Ivy through the kitchen, past a wide stairway, and into a living room equally charming. Western art hung on the walls above over-stuffed leather-upholstered furniture adorned with brass studs. A functional fireplace upon one wall sported a heavy oak mantel and black iron grates.

The taxidermy head of a white buffalo looked down at her from above the mantel. A large ceiling fan spun lazily over the center of the room, circulating the air. Beautiful antique hurricane lamps adorned oak end tables, and a bronze statue of a Pony Express rider sat in the center of the matching coffee table. The largest grandfather clock Ivy had ever seen ticked on another wall. Ivy had a difficult time taking it all in.

They passed a room filled by an ornate desk and bookshelves packed with leather-bound books. Ivy presumed it to be Carl's home office. The blue glow of a computer screen illuminated the room.

At the end of the hall, Carl led her into a bedroom that transported Ivy back a hundred years in time. A massive iron four-poster bed sat in the center of one wall. Across from the bed stood an eight-foot-tall Victorian wardrobe with acid-etched mirrors set into the doors.

Oval braided rugs lay on the marble floors on either side of the big bed—more hurricane lamps with bright green cut-glass shades set upon the oak nightstands. An oak washstand with a large, ornately painted pitcher and bowl stood next to the window hung with floor-to-ceiling lace sheers flanked by rich red velvet drapes, matching the gold tasseled-bedspread and pillow shams.

"Carl, this is beautiful. Did you decorate it yourself?"

Ivy peeked into the adjoining bath decorated with oval miniature portraits, lace curtains, and a large porcelain clock between the double sinks. More oval rugs lay before the tub and sink, and rich Egyptian-cotton towels hung from the black iron towel bars. The rooms were breathtaking.

"Don't you think a man can decorate?" Carl chuckled, but Ivy could tell he appreciated her admiration of his beautiful home. "You should see the playroom upstairs."

Ivy raised an eyebrow. "Not like Christian Grey's playroom, I hope."

"No," he laughed, "strictly a game room with a billiard table, a felt-topped Faro table, and an old bar I rescued from a saloon in Bisbee that was being torn down. It dates back to the days of the Earp brothers, and the boys might have bellied up to it back in the day."

"I can't wait to see it. I bet it's amazing. How many rooms are upstairs?"

"Just the playroom and a bath. It's the room over

the garage. There are two bedrooms down here, but I use one for an office. It has a Murphy-bed if I have company who need a place to stay."

"Nice. Keeps the freeloading relatives away if they think you only have one bedroom," Ivy laughed, still taking in the ornate details of the artwork in the rooms.

Ivy knew her antiques, and Carl had thousands of dollars in decor displayed here. The porcelain pitcher and bowl might have looked like a reproduction to an untrained eye, but the delicate, nearly translucent quality told Ivy it was of actual eighteenth or early nineteenth century German manufacture with ground alabaster mixed with the clay and fired to give a fine translucent glass-like quality. The rich colors of the painted scenes attested to fine hands in a precision artisan's workshop.

"Where did you find all these things, Carl? It's amazing." The grandfather clock chimed a deep, booming gong from the living room. "That clock must have cost a small fortune. I've never seen one that big."

"The clock came from an auction in Austin. It used to stand in the Texas statehouse. It dates back to the beginning of the Republic and came from Germany. It didn't cost as much as that pitcher and bowl if you can believe that. I got that from an auction at the Vanderbilt Mansion."

Ivy touched the delicate bowl with reverence. "I can believe that. It's German, too, right?"

"You *do* know your antiques," Carl said with a raised eyebrow. "Did you see the miniatures in the bathroom?"

"Yes, they're real French miniatures and not reproductions. I'd guess late eighteenth century."

"You'd be correct. They came from a house in

the Garden District in New Orleans. It was an old French family that came over after the Revolution. The one in France, not the one here."

"Did the porcelain clock in there come from the same place?"

"Yes, I wanted to keep them together. You certainly *do* know your antiques."

"I had a house full of them once. None as pricy as these, but I've done some studying on the subject for my books." She smiled. "I keep up my subscription to *Country Living*."

"I know you do. Would you care to join me in the bed? It's not old. I had it custom made by a welder friend of mine to fit my California king mattress."

"They didn't make beds nearly this big back in the day. They could have fit a family of five or six in a bed this big," Ivy laughed and dropped onto the firm pillow-topped mattress. "Feels comfy." She kicked off her shoes and fell back onto the pillows while Carl walked over and switched off the light. She wiggled out of her pants, stripped off her tank top, and pulled back the bedspread and sheet. "Join me?" she teased in the glow of the nightlight from the bathroom.

3

They rose early, showered off the sweat residue from their lovemaking the night before, and dressed. The Lexus pulled out of the drive promptly at five. A coffee stop at the first McDonald's drive-thru was the only interruption of the morning as they made their way to the I-17 north out of the Valley of the Sun toward the I-40 at Flagstaff. That would take them all the way into Oklahoma City, where they'd change to the I-44 North to Tulsa.

It would be a long day's drive, but with good weather and no traffic delays, they could make it easily before midnight.

"I don't know why you don't simply fly to these things," Ivy said as the car made its transition onto the I-40 and the morning sun flashed into her face. She lowered the visor to shield her eyes from the blinding glare.

"I enjoy the solitude of driving, and you don't get this scenery from a plane." Ivy had already heard these explanations before. "Having the car gives me more latitude. If I flew to Tulsa and then decided I wanted to take my girl on up to Branson for a few days, I'd be shit out of luck." He looked over at her and grinned.

"Cheshire would kill me if I left him to my sister's tender mercies for an extended trip to Branson." Ivy gave him a nervous chuckle. "If you wanted to visit Bass Pro Shop, there's one in Mesa now, or are you a closet Donnie and Marie fan?"

"I'm just saying the car gives me more flexibility in my schedule. I like to scout the real estate possibilities when I travel, and rental cars are a pain in the ass. Having my own car is more convenient." He pulled off the highway and into a truck stop to fill the tank. "Why don't you run in and take a pee while I fill up. We won't be stopping again until we hit New Mexico."

Ivy did as he directed and found the ladies' room, walking through the store past aisles of knockoff native artwork made in China. She stopped at the counter on the way out and bought them two more coffees.

She passed Carl on her way out, and he winked at her thoughtfulness. Ivy hated setting the cups on the roof of the expensive automobile, but it was the only option that enabled her to get the door open and back into her seat. She transferred the cups of hot liquid into the cup holders and strapped into the seat belt.

It had been a while since she'd been on a road trip, and she had to admit she was enjoying it. She'd never traveled any farther than from her apartment to a restaurant or a movie theatre with Carl, and she found herself strangely nervous in his expensive automobile. She worried they would run out of topics for discussion and he'd find her boring after all.

Ivy gave a start when his door opened, and Carl slid into the driver's seat of the immaculate vehicle. It still had that new-car smell, though Ivy knew he'd bought it almost two years ago. He smoked cigars in it, and she wondered how he kept it smelling so fresh.

"Thanks for the coffee, baby. I was going to get us some more when I went in." He started the engine, and the cold air from the fan hit Ivy in the face. They didn't really need the air conditioning at this altitude in the early morning, and the warm cup of coffee felt good in Ivy's hands.

"You read my mind." He picked up his cup, popped the little access point on the lid, and sipped. "Off we go." He replaced the cup in the holder, put the car in gear, and returned to the highway.

The high desert of Arizona, flushed by the rising sun, was beautiful. Potash mountains covered in silver-green junipers made up the scenery to the north of them, and vast expanses of sage-covered fields dotted with herds of elk and antelope lay to the south. Navajo hogans with satellite dishes and new pickup trucks were the only signs of human inhabitants marring the pristine beauty of the high-desert landscape.

Carl found a news station on the radio that droned on about the latest wrangling in Congress or terrorists in the Middle East. Ivy tuned it out to soak up the beauty of the passing landscape and daydreamed about the days when men and women in covered wagons being chased by wild Indians or desperados first traversed the virgin countryside.

She wondered what the inside of one of those octagonal Native log dwellings looked like. She'd always dreamed of living in a remote cabin but thought she'd prefer one in the mountains to one in the treeless plains of the rocky desert. Junked tractors and pickups ruined the romance of the Old West when they passed the present-day Native dwellings, and it saddened Ivy to see it.

The only things remotely Old West about the places were the occasional stockade of horses with saddles draped over the wooden rails of the fencing.

"What are you thinking about so intently over there?" Carl asked and switched the radio to an easy-listening station. "You haven't said a word in over an hour."

"I was just enjoying the scenery and letting you listen to the news." Ivy drained her cooled coffee from the Styrofoam cup. "It's so beautiful up here."

"Yes, if it weren't for the fact it gets so cold up here in the winter and all the land is reservation, it would be built up like the valley." He cracked his window and lit a cigar. "You don't mind, do you?"

"Of course not. It's your car." She did mind, but as she said, it was his car, and she was just tagging along.

"I know the smoke bothers your eyes and sinuses."

"It's fine as long as you have the window cracked," Ivy said reassuringly. "What sort of property are you looking at in Tulsa? Student housing?"

"Oh, Lord, no," he said with a grimace. "I'm looking at places to rent out to guest lecturers at the university and visiting parents. Student housing is too labor-intensive. They leave the places a mess or get raided by the police for illegal activities, and I don't need that sort of bullshit."

"That makes sense. So tell me about this lecture you're giving."

He cleared his throat. "It's about the importance of studying the comparable sales in a market area in order to make your best deal when buying or selling a property." He took a long draw on his cigar. "Do you understand what comps are?"

"Of course. Is the name of your lecture 'Studying Comps: Using other people's good or bad luck in the market to enhance your position'?" Ivy asked, a little miffed that he took her for a moron.

"That's a good one," he chuckled. "You understand real estate?"

"I've bought and sold a few houses in my lifetime, and I've been listening to you talk about it for almost a year now." Ivy opened her purse and popped a peppermint candy into her mouth, self-conscious of her bad breath after drinking a cup of coffee.

"It *has* been a year, hasn't it? I didn't realize." Ivy couldn't tell if he actually felt bad about not having kept track of their time together or if he only wanted her to think he was.

Am I being unfair to him? Am I being unfair to myself? If I can't trust how he feels about me, should I even consider continuing a relationship? Am I being ridiculous?

"It's okay, Carl. You have a lot of things on your plate." She watched for a relieved expression on his face. "I don't expect you to keep track of our comings and goings."

"But it's important to *you*. I know it is. Women expect men to show up with candy and flowers on anniversaries." He exhaled a mouth full of sweet white smoke. "I'm sorry, baby."

"Do I really strike you as the candy and flowers type?"

"Wine and jewelry, then?"

"Yeah, right." Ivy rolled her eyes, gave him a slight smile, and wrinkled her nose. "I've never asked for more than your time and your honesty. Candy would make me fat. Flowers die. Wine would be nice, but I don't go anyplace to wear jewelry anymore. It would be a waste of money."

"You're my kind of woman, Ivy Chandler." Carl reached over and squeezed her knee. "We should have done this before. It's nice having someone to chat with."

"I've been trying to tell you that. I'm excellent company, and I'm potty trained."

He laughed. "Do you have a new project?" he asked, referring to her attempt at a career as an author.

"I'm still working on that family epic I was telling you about. I've got the outline and the first three chapters done of the third book. You know I have the first two finished. I've been trying to pitch the project to some agents, but you know how that shit goes." She shrugged her shoulders in mock despair. "I have a hundred rejection e-mails on file."

"Frustrating, isn't it?" Carl had written two books about real estate investing that he'd paid to have published by a vanity press after he couldn't find a traditional publisher or agent for the projects.

"Yes, it is. I'll probably just self-publish again or go with a small press. I wish I had the money to invest in a publicist."

"Yikes. You're talking big money there, baby."

"I know, and it's why I don't have one." Ivy snorted a laugh before turning back to the scenery passing outside her window. "I think I've seen more antelope and elk this trip than I ever have." She watched the twitching tails on several of the white behinds of the graceful creatures standing in the high grasses as they passed.

"I think they've changed the hunting laws on the reservations to conserve the animals." A strong crosswind struck the Lexus, and Carl's knuckles whitened on the steering wheel. "Damned winds are always bad across here." Ivy noted that the speedometer began to fall below seventy-five for the first time since leaving the truck stop that morning. They heard a siren, and a state trooper flew by them on the left with his lights flashing.

"Must be an accident up ahead," Ivy said and readjusted her behind in the seat while checking the security of her seatbelt across her breasts.

"Not uncommon. Big rigs get caught by these crosswinds and go over all the time, or fools in motorhomes who aren't used to driving."

When they came upon the accident, it was a large motorhome blown over on its side off the left lane in the median. The squad car and four civilian cars had pulled up alongside and assisted a bloodied, white-haired woman in climbing out through the open door in the center of the overturned coach. Ivy didn't see any smoke and wondered if the woman had been driving or if another passenger remained inside. An ambulance arrived from the east and crossed the rocky median to park close to the overturned rig.

"They'll be alright now," Carl assured her but kept both hands tight upon the steering wheel and his eyes upon the road for the next several miles.

4

Their trip on into Tulsa proved to be uneventful. They stopped for food and refueling in Grants, New Mexico. Ivy was more than ready to stretch her legs by then and relieve her bladder. She welcomed the toasted turkey sandwich and fries at the Denny's, as well.

They didn't stop again until Amarillo, Texas, where they fueled at a Love's and got some more coffee. Ivy hoped she'd be able to sleep after so much caffeine, but by the time they stopped, she didn't think it would prove to be a problem.

They breezed through Oklahoma City well after the rush-hour traffic but began to hit patches of rain. By the time they reached the Tulsa Clarion, it was half-past midnight, and they'd been driving through a blinding, windswept downpour for almost two hours. Both their nerves were shot. Ivy was glad she hadn't been the one doing the driving. She hated driving after dark, but the addition of the heavy rain and wind would have been impossible for her. Carl met the task stoically, but she tried to keep the conversation to a minimum to avoid distracting him.

They pulled up under the canopied entrance of the big hotel, and Carl popped the gear shift into park. "Well, here we are," he sighed with relief. "I'll go get us checked in if you want to wait here."

"Sounds good to me, but I'll probably step out to stretch a bit. I've been sitting here with a clenched asshole for the past two hours. I need to stand up and walk around."

"Well, I'll grab the bags, and you can just come on in with me then." He sounded tired and exasperated with her.

Ivy opened the door, and a blast of cool, damp wind hit her face. Lightning flashed, and thunder boomed in the night sky. The sound of heavy rain falling on the pavement around them intensified.

Ivy joined Carl at the rear of the car and grabbed her smaller bag that sat upon her larger one next to his. He hefted out the two larger cases and pulled up their extending handles to roll across the covered drive and into the quiet, dimmed lobby of the lovely hotel. Large potted plants stood before every window beside modern Southwestern furniture. Ornately framed Western scenes hung on the walls. The bronze bust of a Native sat upon a pedestal between the two sets of elevator doors.

It surprised Ivy as people began streaming into the lobby from the stairwells, most looking bleary-eyed as if just being awakened and wearing their robes and slippers or hastily thrown-on street clothes.

"I'm sorry to inconvenience you folks," a heavy-set balding man in a cheap maroon polyester jacket with a brass tag with Manager etched into it announced, "but we're under a tornado alert, and I have to ask all of you to follow Joanna back to the pool area until we get the all-clear from the authorities." He pointed to a slim, young woman of Native

American roots, wearing a matching polyester jacket.

Carl inched his way to the counter through complaining patrons to be told they couldn't be checked in because the computers were down due to the storm. The girl at the counter told him to join the others heading to the pool area and that he could leave his car under the canopy for the time being.

They followed the crowd of grumbling men, women, and children down a hall until they came to a broad set of metal doors indicating the pool. Joanna pushed them open and secured them with a wedge. Ivy heard rain and hail pelting the glass ceiling covering the pool area and looked at Carl in the glow of the intermittent flashes of lightning.

"Why would they bring us here for a tornado?" Ivy gasped, looking up at the glass panels above their heads and involuntarily ducking with every loud crack of thunder.

"I don't know, baby." He took her hand. "It must be set up with the state or something."

"It doesn't feel that safe to me," Ivy said, warily glancing up at the panels above their heads.

Others were harshly raising the same questions to their young guide, Joanna, who seemed to be on the verge of tears. Ivy couldn't tell whether the girl was more afraid of the storm or the crowd of angry people barking at her.

"I'm sorry, folks, but this is the designated storm safety area for the hotel. We have to stay in here until the all-clear is sounded by the county. We've been assured that these Plexiglas panels are set into reinforced steel and are the safest place to be during a storm. This room rode out the last two big ones with no damage whatsoever," she said in a reassuring tone.

Ivy looked up as heavier hail pelted the panels, and she stepped closer to Carl when a drop of water fell onto her face from above. "The damned ceiling's leaking," Ivy said loudly, wiping the cold drop of water from her cheek. Through the fogging Plexiglas windows around the pool enclosure, Ivy saw trees being whipped around violently, and hail the size of golf balls beat down and bounced off the cars in the parking lot.

Something big struck one of the panels above their heads. Ivy heard a distinct cracking sound and soon saw and heard debris falling into the water of the nearby pool. Carl tugged her into the planter close to the stone wall as women and children screamed and ran for the doors and out into the hall.

Ivy watched as grown men trampled on fallen children in their haste to exit the pool area where other panels had begun to fall in a cascading sequence, one after the other, onto the concrete floor of the supposedly safe room. Hailstones, rain, and hotel patrons fell into the pool and over the metal patio furniture.

Carl pulled her down into a squatting position amongst the banana trees and birds of paradise planted along the decorative flagstone wall. He huddled over her, protecting her from flying shards of Plexiglas and the floundering arms of people as they rushed by, screaming and cursing.

Carl only left her side once to pull a dazed and bleeding Joanna, who clutched a sobbing little girl, from the floor and into the planter next to them.

"Get on in here with us, girls, and stay close to the wall with your heads covered." He took off his sweater and wrapped it around the shivering, sobbing child in Joanna's arms. Seconds later, a panel crashed to the floor where the two had once huddled, shattering into a thousand jagged pieces. Ivy flinched as a few shards flew up into their hiding space.

Ivy jumped every time a panel came crashing to the floor. "I bet this will be the *last* time you invite *me* on a trip," Ivy whispered into Carl's ear as he held her amongst the dripping, beaten foliage.

"Bullshit," he said and gulped, tightening his grip. "If I'd stopped when you wanted me to an hour ago, we'd have missed this. I should have listened to you."

The storm abated a few minutes after Carl had pulled Joanna and the child into the planter. They stepped out into a mass of carnage and destruction. Joanna handed the wailing child off to Ivy while she and Carl assisted people downed around the pool area. In the glow of emergency lights, Ivy could see blood pooled upon the textured concrete littered with shattered Plexiglas. Men and women sat rocking weeping children and one another.

The screams and wails of humans gave way to those of emergency vehicles' sirens, and soon men in the gold canvas jackets of firefighters tended to the injured. Joanna led Carl and Ivy to the front desk, where she found them keycards to a room.

"You'll have to take the stairs up because the elevators are shut off, but I put you in a room on the second floor."

Carl reached for his wallet. "What do we owe you, miss?"

Joanna pursed her lips. "You don't owe a damned thing, mister. I'll take care of it. If that asshole manager of mine says anything, I'll bust his balls for sure." She took Carl's hand. "Thanks, mister. If it hadn't been for you, me and that kid would be goners."

"How is the little one?" Carl asked as he patted Joanna's shivering hand.

"They took her to the hospital with a broken arm. They finally found her parents hiding in the walk-in cooler in the kitchen with the manager and some others." She huffed and furrowed her dusky-skinned brow. "Bunch of real heroes there."

"You were the hero here tonight, Joanna. You stayed with your guests when everyone else ran and hid. I'll make certain the corporate offices know about it, too, I promise you that. Your manager will not be getting an endorsement, by the way," Carl assured the young woman.

"From me as well," Ivy added.

Before they climbed up the stairs to their room, Carl went out to check on his car. It was okay, but now parked beside it idled a local affiliate's news van. He took the opportunity to advise the reporter with the van about what had occurred, and as they passed back through the lobby, Ivy saw Joanna being interviewed while paramedics bandaged her head wound. Carl gave her a mischievous wink and a smile as they passed.

"That was sweet of you, Carl," Ivy said as she slogged her heavy, damp bag up the stairs.

"The girl deserved to catch a break after all the bullshit she got from people around that pool while her asshole boss hid away in a damned cooler."

"Right, he goes into a reinforced metal box while he sends that kid and us into a leaky glass room. He should be sent to jail." Ivy stood while Carl opened the door to a room that turned out to be an elegant suite with a fully stocked bar and a large basket of fruit on the coffee table.

"Wow," Ivy exclaimed as the regular lights

blinked back on. "This must have been meant for one of the conference VIPs."

"How do you know I'm *not* one of the VIPs?" He laughed and selected a bottle of sweet red wine to open. "You up for a drink before bed?"

Ivy dropped into one of the over-stuffed chairs. "You bet I am," she sighed. "You bet I am."

5

The annual Tulsa Realtor's Conference had to be canceled due to storm damage in the city of Tulsa. No other hotel could be found in a pinch to transfer the event to. Carl and Ivy enjoyed their lovely suite until the next morning when housekeeping came in and interrupted their shower. They packed up the complimentary fruit basket, a box of Swiss chocolates, and terry robes. They left the key card with housekeeping and took the reopened elevators to the lobby.

The Lexus still sat parked under the canopy, and Ivy had to admit she was happy to be back inside the sturdy car. Carl packed the suitcases into the back and joined her with a smile. He was overjoyed the vehicle had been spared damage by the hail, eyeing the many deep pits in vehicles in the parking lot as they buckled their seatbelts.

"How does dinner in Branson sound, baby?"

"Sounds great to me as long as we stay someplace without an indoor pool," Ivy said with a smile.

"Absolutely, but I need some coffee. How about you?"

"Do you think there's a Waffle House anywhere

close by?" Ivy hated giving away her hillbilly roots like that, but she was hungry, and a pecan waffle and sausage patties sounded good.

Carl took out his phone and typed. "Just up the street if the storm didn't take it out." He started the car and pulled out onto the mud-caked street.

Ivy saw signs everywhere of last night's storm. Hail had pock-marked cars in driveways, people had boarded up broken windows with plywood, and curled sheets of metal roofing littered the ground along the streets.

Ivy really had no desire to see it, but Carl drove around the Clarion to where the haunting structure over the pool stood. They couldn't get too close because the downed limbs of trees blocked the entrance. The hum of chainsaws filled the air as county crews attempted to clear the way.

To Ivy's utter pleasure, the Waffle House stood intact and open for business. With a twenty-four-hour schedule, the staff, on duty since the night before, looked haggard but still met them with smiles as they entered.

"Sit anywhere you like," a thin, older woman with white roots attesting to her dyed-black hair, told them. "Were y'all here for the storm last night?"

"Yes, ma'am, at the Clarion," Carl told her as they sat at a booth being cleared by a dumpy young man in a Waffle House shirt.

She looked at Carl a little closer. "I think I saw you on Channel 6 this morning. Were you in that sunroom that fell in around the pool?"

He took Ivy's hand. "Yes, we were. There's not much of it left now, I'm afraid."

"I heard a bunch of folks got hurt."

"A few cuts and broken bones."

"The news made out like that little gal from the

office was a real hero," the young man said as he poured them coffee and handed them tall single-sheet menus with color pictures of steaks, waffles, and sandwiches printed upon it.

"That she was," Ivy said with enthusiasm. "*She* took us down to that pool area when the manager told her to and stayed there with us when the roof started falling in while the manager hid out in the kitchen's walk-in cooler."

Ivy noticed others in the full restaurant watching her as she spoke. "That girl shielded children with her own little body while the roof caved in, and that fat jerk hid in a cooler."

People around them shook their heads in disgust. "She should get a medal from the city for her bravery, and the company should reward her too. Carl and I are surely writing letters." Ivy saw heads nodding in agreement.

"Joanna Kingfisher is my late husband's niece and a member of our tribe," the old waitress announced proudly. "The tribal council will certainly see to it that she gets the recognition she deserves."

Ivy took a business card from her wallet and handed it to the woman. "If you'll write down who we should write, we'll be happy to supply first-hand testimony to the girl's bravery and heroism."

The woman took Ivy's card in her claw-like fingers and read it. She flipped it over and scribbled something. "Send your letters to this man. He's our tribal president. It says here you're a book writer? You write something good about our Joanna and make it sound good."

"We promise that we will." Ivy smiled and tucked the card back into her wallet. "I'd love a pecan waffle, two eggs scrambled with cheese, and two sausage patties."

"I'll have the same," Carl told her.

Their excellent breakfast continued to be interrupted by people wanting to hear the whole story about their night in the storm. Carl and Ivy laid it on thick, hoping the hotel's fat, white, cowardly manager would have to bear the brunt of malicious gossip. At the same time, they thought, the young Native American girl should be recognized as the hero of the dreadful night's business.

According to one customer, the little girl Joanna had rescued remained in the hospital recovering from her broken arm and the after-effects of shock. Child services were investigating her parents for running off and leaving her as well.

She and Carl found that bit of news enjoyable. How could two adults run off and leave their innocent seven-year-old child the way they had? As a mother and grandmother, Ivy could not fathom it. If she'd lost hold of her child in that melee, she certainly wouldn't have kept moving forward without her.

Back in the car with coffee in to-go cups, they made their way to the highway over litter-strewn streets, past work crews in bright orange jumpsuits, and around downed power lines. As they drove north toward the rolling hills of Missouri, the signs of storm damage disappeared.

Ivy reveled in the cloying green all around her. Mist hung in the hollows between the Ozark Mountains, giving the place an ethereal feel. The Ozarks were one of Ivy's favorite places in the state, and she always enjoyed the drive through the area when she was on her way east to visit family and friends. She stared out the window soaking up the verdant green.

"What you thinking about, baby?" Carl cracked

the window and lit a cigar. "Are you still freaked out about last night?"

"No, I'm just enjoying the trees. It's so unbelievably beautiful here with all the green around us." Ivy picked up her coffee cup but returned it to the holder when she noted it was nearly empty. "Are we due for gas soon? I could use a pee and a refill," she said as she smiled and shook the empty cup.

"It is pretty. Reminds me of home." Carl had come from Wisconsin, while Ivy had grown up in southern Indiana. She smiled when John Mellencamp came on the radio. Unlike other Hoosiers, Ivy had never been a fan, and she'd caught grief for it in the past.

"Can we lose the 'Pink Houses'?" she asked, and he switched the channel to the news station where the announcer droned on about storm damage sustained in Oklahoma overnight.

"This isn't much better," he laughed and found a classic rock channel playing Lynyrd Skynyrd's 'Free Bird.' "Here we go."

It was just after two when they got into Branson, Missouri, where the main street teemed with men, women, and children in summer clothes and flip-flops. They flocked into the many tourist traps lining the street.

Carl pulled into a Howard Johnson's, and they went in to register. The building was old. Ivy suspected it had been initially erected in the early seventies when Branson had come into its own as a Midwestern tourist destination. While Carl registered, Ivy went through the brochures advertising music events at the various theatres and boating excursions on Lake of the Ozarks, the town's original big draw. The music halls had sprung up as enticement for the fishermen to include their wives and children on their visits to the lake or the Current River.

"They had to put us on the third floor," Carl grumbled. "The place is practically booked up."

"Tourist season," Ivy chided. "You probably should have called ahead and made reservations."

"You're probably right. You should be my travel coordinator." He laughed and took Ivy's hand as they entered the elevator that took them slowly to the top floor. The carpet smelled musty with stale tobacco smoke. Ivy noted how dated the room looked with the mauve and blue wallpaper popular in the mid-eighties, the matching drapes on the window, and bedspreads on the two queen-size beds. Narrow brass frames surrounded prints of irises and lilacs, confirming Ivy's dating of the décor.

"You'd think they'd update these rooms more than every forty years," Carl complained as he picked up the square plastic ice bucket and headed to the door. "Gonna get some ice. You want a Coke from the machine?"

"Sure, but make it a root beer or something fruity. I'm overloaded with caffeine."

"Okay, I got ya."

He left, and Ivy began shaking out her clothes to hang on the rack by the door. She shook them out well before hanging them as they'd gotten damp in last night's storm. She hoped they wouldn't smell musty after being trapped in the damp bag overnight and most of the day.

Carl returned with the plastic container filled with ice and two cans of Orange Crush. "Thanks, sweetie." She took one of the cans of soda, popped it open, and took a drink. "You better get your things out of the suitcases. Mine are a little damp."

"Good Lord," he sighed, "I never even thought

about that." He unzipped his bag and began leafing through his neatly folded clothes. "Mine are dry," he said with relief.

"My bags are just cheap shit," she said, embarrassed, and hung her final skirt. "These will be fine in an hour or two with the ceiling fan on."

6

They enjoyed a lazy afternoon watching television and making love. Carl ordered a pizza from the local Papa John's and got more sodas from the machine in the hall.

"Do you want to go to a show tonight?" he asked as they finished their pie. "I think I saw Donnie and Marie on one of the marquees." Carl laughed when he saw Ivy grimace. "The Oak Ridge Boys, then?"

"That's alright. I'm enjoying spending a quiet night after all the driving and the excitement of last night." Ivy swallowed the last of her soda. "Let's just stay in tonight and start fresh in the morning." She watched him leaf through a local real estate magazine he'd picked up in the lobby. "You planning to mix some business with pleasure?"

"I noticed a few vacation condos and properties listed in here that I thought we might take a look at while we're here. Are you interested in getting into the real estate game?"

Ivy snorted a soft chuckle. "With what? My stunning good looks and witty charm? I don't think I could manage financing with that." She laughed, let her robe fall from her shoulders, and strode through the room to the bathroom where she turned on the hot water in the shower.

"I'm going to soak for a bit. I ache all over." Ivy stepped into the white porcelain tub and let the hot water drench her hair and aching body. She reached for the bottle of shampoo and lathered her brunette waves. The hot water felt marvelous. She rinsed the suds from her hair and added cream rinse. While she let the conditioner do its thing, Ivy lathered her body, attending to all her crevices until she felt clean and refreshed. She put her head back under the jet and rinsed out the creamy conditioner until her fingers ran smoothly through her shoulder-length hair.

As she was about to turn off the shower, hands pulled open the plastic curtain, and Carl joined her. "You all clean now, baby? Ready to get dirty again?" He bit her playfully on her exposed shoulder and reached for a breast. Carl pulled her hand around to rest upon his firm erection. "I'm ready again."

"You're a horn-dog." She laughed and squeezed his stiff erection. "You sure you're up for another round today?"

"I am if you are. You keep me up, baby." He nudged at her behind with his hard cock, and she backed up into him, the water washing over them from above, beginning to cool.

Carl ran his hands over her wet body, massaging her sore back and shoulders. "That feels so good," she cooed.

"I have something that's going to feel even better." He chuckled and nudged her behind with his erection. She rolled her eyes, knowing what he had in mind for her. Ivy braced herself with both arms upon the wall below the shower nozzle while Carl rubbed the head of his erection into the crack between her ass cheeks, looking for the point of entry there. It wasn't Ivy's favorite position, but she knew how much he enjoyed it and obliged him.

"You know what I like, baby," he whispered into her ear under the running water of the shower. His hands kneaded the cheeks of her shapely behind, slowly pulling them apart and inching his cock into place over her tight anus. "Ease it up now, baby, and let me in," he breathed into her ear.

She winced as he entered but moaned ever so quietly to make him think she enjoyed his attentions there.

"Is that okay, baby? I'll stop if it hurts," he whispered, but he continued pushing into her. Ivy knew that regardless of his quiet words, Carl wouldn't have stopped if she'd said it hurt. Once he'd gained entry into his favorite orifice, there was no stopping him.

"Go ahead, sweetie," she said, pushing back into his thrust. "Give it to me the way you like it."

"Oh, baby, you're too good to me." He pushed into her until Ivy could feel his heavy balls bouncing off her wet ass cheeks with every ardent thrust. She bit her lips with the pain as he stretched the orifice but allowed him to finish and have his pleasure. It never took long that way, and Ivy enjoyed hearing his moans of delight in her ear. "Oh God, baby, here it comes." He bellowed and thrust deep one final time with his release.

His hands slipped from her cheeks as his wilting erection slipped from her anal embrace. He rested his head, panting, upon her shoulder. "I need to get under the water now, baby." The water had cooled, and Carl let the cold spray wash over his sweaty body and bright white hair. "You treat me like no other woman ever has, Ivy Chandler. You're amazing."

Ivy rolled her eyes at his empty words. "Thanks, sweetie." She used a soapy washcloth to wipe him from her tender crack gently then stepped out of the tub to dry her body with one of the flimsy, motel-issue towels. She wrapped her head in another and moved a dry, folded towel on the rack for Carl to quickly grab on his way out of the shower. She stepped from the cold tile of the bathroom and cringed as her bare foot stepped onto the stiff old low-pile carpet of the bedroom. The place needed a serious makeover.

Ivy heard him turn off the shower, and the plastic curtain was pushed aside. A few minutes later, the toilet flushed, and Carl joined her back on the bed in front of the television buzzing with an old Clint Eastwood spaghetti Western.

"That was awesome, baby." He fell back upon the pillows piled in front of the headboard bolted to the wall above the mattress. "We're gonna do this more often."

"You promise?" Ivy asked, hopefully.

"I promise." He bent and kissed her mouth. "I think I'm gonna nap for a bit now." He snuggled into her shoulder, and soon, Ivy heard his soft, even snores.

He promises, but I'm not going to be holding my breath. After last night I bet this is a one-and-done trip.

Ivy picked up the discarded real estate magazine Carl had been reading before their shower. She looked at the different ads he'd circled. One was listed as a hunting retreat on twelve private, partially wooded acres for four hundred thousand dollars; another was a two-level log cabin on five acres next to Forest Service property that promised unlimited turkey for two hundred and fifty thousand.

The one that piqued Ivy's interest was a two-bedroom single-level log cabin on two acres with a working fireplace for one seventy-five. It sat in a picturesque clearing with an Irish setter in the manicured green yard. Ivy was certain the dog was not included in the price and smiled. She saw a few condos on the lake marked, as well.

It looks as though he does have a big day planned for us tomorrow.

From the nightstand bolted to the wall, Ivy picked up her laptop. She booted it up and checked her e-mail. She rolled her eyes when she saw ninety-nine plus marked for her inbox. Most would be junk, but she needed to check because she expected word from the editor for her first round of edits on her latest romance novel. Historical fiction was Ivy's passion, but the erotica she had published by a small press actually paid a little.

Ivy hated this part of the process. Editors always wanted her to change things. Sometimes the changes made sense, but other times they were stupid changes like the color of a character's hair or eyes. Continuity changes made sense, but why change having the character come from Irish ancestry to Norwegian? Take out this word or that because a reader might find it offensive. She had written it to *be* offensive because the situation or time period called for it. Ivy tended to make the changes without much fuss but griped and grumbled about it privately.

Ivy scanned the list of mail. There was nothing from her publisher, but she did have a message from an agent she'd queried. Another rejection, no doubt. She opened it with trepidation.

Dear Ms. Chandler,

Thank you for your interest in our agency. While we seldom represent your genre, we found your first few pages and your synopsis intriguing. Please

forward us the first three chapters of your manuscript for further review.
The Strider Agency

Well, that was encouraging. Ivy had yet to get that far with a literary agency before. She had a whole file filled with cordial rejection letters to prove it. Hurriedly cutting and pasting the first three chapters of the first book in her series into an e-mail, Ivy replied with thanks for the agency's kind consideration of her work. On impulse, she went back and added the first three chapters of the second book, as well. It couldn't hurt. Then she went to her blog and passed along the happy news to her few followers.

She found it unfortunate, but shameless self-promotion was a big part of the writing game these days. Ivy often wondered if Charles Dickens and Mark Twain had dealt with the same problems. At least she had the internet.

Carl slept for an hour while she went through her e-mail, reading blogs she followed, but for the most part, deleting spam from people trying to sell her internet promotions. Ivy wished she could take advantage of more of them, but fifty dollars here and fifty dollars there added up quickly. She had a couple of monthly promotions she used as well as her website upkeep, but that was about as much as she could afford at the moment.

Most writers go into it thinking they're going to write the Great American Novel, get discovered, and start raking in the big royalty checks. In reality, it rarely happened that way. First-time authors seldom saw big money. Ivy knew she would have to kiss a lot of frogs before finding a prince if there were actually any princes left out there.

She loved writing, and it occupied her dreary hours at home. She had stories to tell and would keep it up as long as her fingers continued to work, or until her mind gave out.

In Ivy's mind, getting rich and famous was not as important to her as having her work become popular with readers. Like most fledgling authors, Ivy fantasized about her books becoming feature films someday, but she tended to be a realist and knew that was more than likely a fantasy.

Carl roused at her side. "You writing, baby?" He stretched and yawned. "You writing about my amazing sexual prowess?"

"Just answering some e-mails."

"Any good news?" He threw his bare legs over the edge of the bed, stood, and walked into the bathroom.

"I got an e-mail from one of those literary agencies I queried in New York. They wanted to see the first three chapters." Ivy shut down and closed her laptop.

"That's great, baby," he said over the flushing of the toilet. "Maybe you're on your way to being able to support me in the style to which I could become accustomed." He laughed and trudged back to the bed. "What are you going to do?"

"I sent them the first three chapters of both manuscripts. I'm not going to hold my breath, though."

"Don't be that way, baby." He leaned over and pecked her on the cheek. "You've been hoping for just this sort of opportunity for as long as I've known you. Be positive." He rolled over and pulled the light blanket up over his shoulders to settle in for the night.

7

Carl did indeed have a big day planned for them. After a hearty breakfast in the hotel restaurant, they piled into the Lexus and began driving all around the wooded countryside. They met two different realtors who showed them several properties.

A condo on the lake with a private boat dock particularly impressed Carl. Ivy wasn't as impressed. Its decor was ultra-modern, and it turned her country stomach. The art on the walls looked as though it had been done in a preschool, and Ivy thought the abstract metal sculpture would have received a failing grade in any welding class.

Carl tried to look nonchalant, but Ivy could tell he was very taken with the beautiful view of the boats on the lake and the surrounding green mountains.

"Lovely view," Ivy said as she took his hand at the wide window overlooking a set of fast boats pulling water skiers. "Noisy, but nice."

The realtor regaled them with the opportunities the private dock below offered and how much they'd enjoy visiting here while others suffered the hot summers in Arizona.

Ivy walked away to look at the tiny kitchen once more and asked if she could use the bathroom. The heavy, balding realtor told her yes, and she went into the even tinier guest bath. When she came out, she made a point of going to stand by the door to let Carl know she'd seen enough.

They went on to one other condo that Ivy saw more potential in but was still not bowled over by. After the condos, they traveled down some narrow asphalt roads to look at hunting properties and cabins. Eventually, they drove up to the little log cabin that had been pictured with the dog on the green lawn.

The lawn was overgrown now, and there was no dog. Ivy found the setting quite picturesque with the tall oaks, maples, and sweetgums salted with shorter dogwoods and redbuds amongst the trunks of the bigger trees. Ivy could imagine the beauty in the spring when the shorter trees would be in full bloom. Behind the cabin, Ivy could see a fenced area where someone once maintained a vegetable garden and a small glassed-in greenhouse for starting plants.

A flagstone walk led from the gravel drive to the green tin-roofed porch, fronting the entire cabin. A wooden porch swing suspended by rusty dog chains hung at the far end of the long porch.

"It's charming," Ivy whispered to Carl as he helped her up the railed wooden steps.

"I knew you'd like this one," he whispered back and gently rubbed the small of her back as she turned and glanced around at the green countryside beyond the cabin.

The charm continued inside with a substantial river-rock fireplace, weathered pine planking on the floors, a deep ceramic farm-sink, and a retooled antique cooking stove in the roomy kitchen. Ivy thought she'd been transported back a hundred years to a nineteenth-century pioneer's homestead. She fell in love with the rustic cabin at first sight.

Less impressed, Carl asked about plumbing, wiring, emergency services, and zoning codes. Ivy thought he was looking for an excuse not to be impressed. Ivy, however, could find none.

The realtor tried some pressure tactics when he thought they might be buyers, telling them he had two other offers on the property. Carl ignored this ploy and continued out to the utility room where a washer and dryer sat next to an old galvanized washtub set up as a deep sink for pre-washing. A clothesline with wooden pins still clipped to it swung in the light breeze beyond the back door.

"How much is this one listed for?" Carl asked as they stepped back out onto the front porch. A pickup came bouncing up the road. The driver honked and waved as he passed.

"One seventy-five," the realtor replied, "but I think they have offers up to two twenty-five already. It's a good property for summer rentals, especially if you fit it with bunks in the two bedrooms and a sleeper sofa in the living room. A person could set it up to rent out to as many as six or eight."

"Not with only one bath," Carl huffed.

"Another bath could be added easily enough off the second bedroom." The realtor shrugged.

"Is this on a well and septic or city utilities?" Ivy asked.

"A good sweet well that taps right into the local aquifer and a septic tank that's been pumped regular. The house is only twenty years old."

"Hmm." Ivy nodded and sat in the porch swing. "How far is it from the river? Any flooding problems in the area? I noticed some washed-out areas along the road as we drove in."

The realtor gave her an odd look but pointed toward the south. "It floods some down that way in the spring, but never up this far, and if it does, the roads are usually clear to drive through in a matter of a few hours."

The realtor cleared his throat and tried to change the subject. "The river everyone uses for tubing passes three miles from here. That's why this place would be perfect for advertising in sporting and vacation magazines. It's close to the tubing station on the river and the lake."

"No problems with pesticide runoff into the aquifer then? I see lots of bean fields around here," Ivy persisted.

"No, ma'am, most of the farmers use the GMO seed now and don't need to use pesticides."

Ivy stood and joined Carl walking toward the car. She took his hand, and he squeezed it warmly, giving her a wink and an appreciative smile.

"Thanks for your time," Carl told him. "I have your card, and we'll be in touch." They got into the car and left the realtor standing in the knee-high grass, looking disgruntled.

"He thought he had a sale." Carl smirked. "Those were some good questions about the groundwater and flooding. Really threw him off his game."

"He didn't expect educated questions from a silly woman, I suppose." Ivy chuckled as she buckled her seatbelt. "Typical chauvinist prick."

"Yes, exactly." Carl glanced at her, but Ivy thought she saw a spark of newfound respect in his bright blue eyes. "Did you like that place? It sort of looked like every cowboy cabin you write about right down to the wood-burning cookstove in the kitchen."

"The only thing missing was the smelly outhouse, but we could build one of those." Ivy laughed, bent, and took two bottled waters from the cooler at her feet. "You liked the condo on the lake better, didn't you?"

"As an investment, but not to live in myself. The condo with the private boat slip is a perfect investment property here. It has three bedrooms, two baths, and could be set up to accommodate as many as ten fishermen."

"It would take a long time to get a return on your investment at almost half a million."

"Not really, a place like that would rent for up to three grand a week, and with the proper promotion, you could probably keep it full for twenty weeks a year. It would pay for itself in a couple of years with good management."

"You'd have to find a good local management company."

"Or move here and manage it myself."

"What?" Ivy asked, looking at him aghast. "You'd leave Arizona?"

"I spend most of the summers away from Arizona now. I thought we might spend three seasons here and the winters back in Arizona. This would be a nice central base of operations for my other properties, and we both like the area." Carl took out a cigar and lit it.

"We?" she asked, stupefied, and took a long drink of her water.

"You're always complaining about not having a steady income," he said in a matter-of-fact tone, "I thought I could set you up in an office here, and you could take reservations and arrange for cleaning and stuff. I'd pay you a salary."

It made her happy that he was thinking of her,

but it surprised Ivy that Carl would think she'd be willing to simply pick up and move at the drop of a hat.

"It's certainly something to think about." Ivy took another long pull on the water bottle.

Who the hell does he think he is? Who the hell does he think I am? He thinks I'm some desperate, needy woman who'll just drop everything in her life to move to the sticks and clean his rental properties.

8

Their return trip to Arizona proved to be quiet and uneventful. The weather remained clear, and the Lexus had no problems. Ivy found herself counting down the miles as they got closer to the valley and was happy to drop onto her comfy sofa and cuddle with Cheshire when she finally got home a week and a half after leaving with Carl for Tulsa.

Strained conversations had peppered their trip back, and Ivy could tell she'd confused Carl with her long silences. He'd made her a generous offer of employment and an opportunity to spend more time with him. Carl must have assumed that was what Ivy wanted and could not understand her pensiveness and lack of gratitude.

"I've obviously insulted you somehow," Carl said after he dropped her bags on the floor in her bedroom. "It's certainly not what I intended."

"I'm not insulted, sweetie." She reached for his hand as he passed her on the couch. "I appreciate the thought, but I don't know that I want to pick up and move to Missouri without giving it some very careful thought."

"Well, of course, you don't. You need to talk it over with your family, and you've got this place." He swept his hand to indicate her apartment. "When is your lease up here?"

She thought for a minute. "Four months, but the new management company told us we could break the lease as long as we gave them a thirty-day notice. They have a long waiting list for tenants here."

"That's good. It will take some time to get the financing settled on the condos anyhow."

"Condos as in both the units we looked at?" Ivy asked with a raised eyebrow.

"In for a penny, in for a pound," he said, grinning. "They both have the same potential, and the second one was considerably less expensive than the first. The return on the investment would be quicker. I'm going to look into some reservation software I read about.

"I'll e-mail you the info, and you can check it out, and if you don't mind, contact some of those magazines I stuck in your bag about their advertising rates and packages. Check out the ads in them and see if anything appeals to you. You're a writer. I bet you can come up with some great ad copy to attract renters." He bent and gave her a quick peck on the cheek. "I'll call you tomorrow." He left her sitting with her mouth open.

I feel like a damned secretary already, and we haven't even talked about a salary yet. How long am I expected to do pro bono work before I start getting a paycheck? What the hell am I thinking?

Ivy stood, walked to her room, and began emptying her dirty clothes from the suitcases into her laundry bin. She stared at the mounting pile and knew what she would be filling her day with tomorrow. It would not be the study of software programs or advertising packages. That was for damned sure.

Ivy picked up the bundle of bass fishing and Ozarks vacation rental magazines and slammed them onto the top of her dresser but continued to pitch her clothes into the bin with mounting disgust.

He invites me on a trip and calls it a working vacation, dangles a home in the green mountains and a relationship under my nose, and hints at a salaried position along with a pile of work. Mom always said that rich men didn't get rich by passing their cash around freely. She also said no man would buy the cow if he was already getting the milk for free. Maybe I should have paid closer attention to Mom after all.

Feeling disgusted with herself and her choices of late, Ivy stripped and stomped to her shower. Maybe a long, hot soak would clear her head. She stood under the hot spray and let it wash her tears down the drain. She allowed the hot, steamy water to soak away her aches, both mental and physical. Ivy stood basking in the shower until the water began to cool. She finally turned off the water, stepped out onto the rug, and grabbed a towel. She wrapped her dripping hair in one and her curvy body in another.

Back in her room, Ivy plugged in her laptop and pulled up her documents file. She opened her latest manuscript and began rereading her last few chapters, editing as she read. She always found small mistakes this way; missed words, wrong words, or continuity issues.

After midnight she saved her work and logged off. Ivy thought about giving her e-mail a quick check but thought better of it and turned off the machine. It had been a long, tiring day at the end of a long, tiring week. She glanced from the stack of magazines with their promise of a new and unknown future with Carl back to her laptop with all her hours of work and the yet unfulfilled promise of a future as an author.

I should be realistic. I'm nearly sixty years old. What sort of future do I really have as an author? If I go to Missouri with Carl, I can still write and possibly have the relationship I've been hoping for with him.

Ivy closed the machine, set it aside, and fell back onto her pillows. Once he knew the coast was clear and Ivy was no longer working, Cheshire jumped up onto the bed and curled up next to her, purring softly. Ivy dropped her hand to his soft fur and kneaded his belly. He caught her hand with his clawed paws and began biting at her fingers, encouraging her to continue. She did but soon fell asleep to the soft rhythm of his purring.

The next day found Ivy covered up in the dirty laundry. Her apartment smelled of Tide, Downy, and dryer sheets by the middle of the afternoon when she finally put away the last load and opened her laptop for the first time that day. Ivy went into her e-mail file and was surprised to see something from the Strider Literary Agency already. It had only been a week since she'd sent them the requested chapters, and she hadn't expected more than the cursory automatic 'we got your submission' response.

Ivy eagerly pressed the key to open the mail.

Ms. Chandler,

We are happy to inform you that your opening chapters have been well received by our review committee, and they would like to see your two completed manuscripts. If the rest of the manuscripts are as impressive as the opening chapters, I believe we will be able to offer you representation. With that in mind, I am attaching a copy of our standard agreement for you to familiarize yourself with.

We look forward to seeing your manuscripts and possibly working with you as a promising long-term client.

Sincerely,

Janice Strider, President, The Strider Agency

Ivy popped open the attachment and read through the basic legal mumbo jumbo. What it boiled down to was the Strider Agency being entitled to fifteen percent of any profits her book made from royalties or movie rights the agency might arrange.

Ivy quickly hit reply, attached the document files of her manuscripts, and sent it off for their consideration with a hopeful heart. Could it really be this easy? She'd read about such things happening, and even one of the women in her weekly critique group had found representation and received a contract along with a sizeable check for one of her sword-and-sorcery fantasies. Ivy never really thought it would happen to her.

She came back to her senses. It hadn't happened yet. She finished going through her mail, deleting most of it, and thought about doing a little work on her new manuscript. Instead, she opened her blog page and wrote four hundred words about how happy she was to have made it to round three of the Agent Acquisition Battle. She didn't write anything about Branson.

Ivy dedicated her blog to her writing and generally didn't bring up personal matters unless they had some connection to her writing life.

Later this week, she would be doing a podcast

with a friend, and she intended to talk about the events in Tulsa as that story had been in the national headlines, and YouTube had been airing the storm damage non-stop. Her friend told her he could link to photos of the destroyed Clarion's pool area as well as some of the news footage of Joanna and Carl's interviews. No publicity was bad publicity, as the saying went. Ivy was happy to get all that she could. If getting caught in a tornado in Oklahoma could help her sell books about women in the Old West, she'd take it. She also took the time to send a letter to the Clarion people about the spineless manager and the heroic young woman at the hotel that night.

The next six weeks went by unbearably slowly. Carl had gone away on business again with an added few days visiting his grandchildren in Wisconsin on their dairy farm. She rarely heard from him on those trips, and she missed him.

They'd only spoken once between returning from Missouri and his leaving again the following week, and it had been strained. He'd called to see if she'd reviewed the information about the reservation software and made note of her lack of enthusiasm.

"Ivy, if you're not interested in this project, let me know now before I make a huge investment."

"Carl, it's not that I'm not interested," she sighed, "I just have a lot to think about, and you know how I am with technology. It makes me nervous. I'd need to have somebody personally instruct me on using the software before I could feel comfortable with it."

"We can do that, I suppose. Don't they offer a tutorial?" he asked.

"I believe so. I'll look at it again." Ivy picked up her coffee cup and sipped at the cooling brew. "How long are you going to be gone?"

"I'm not certain. I'm going to stop off and see the kids. The baby's birthday is coming up, and they're planning a party." Ivy smiled. She knew his youngest granddaughter was turning six, but he still called her the baby.

"Well, have a good time. They grow up fast. Before you know it they'll be throwing her a sweet sixteen party."

"Don't remind me," he groaned. "Being closer to the kids is one of the reasons I want to make the move to Branson. It would be a nice place to bring them during their summer break from school. Arizona is too damned hot and too far from their mother."

"It would be nice for mine too. You know how much my sons like to hunt and fish."

"So, you *have* been giving it some consideration then?" He sounded relieved.

"Of course I have, sweetie. I'd much rather be sitting in the shade by the lake fishing than cooped up here in this apartment because you take the chance of spontaneously combusting every time you walk out the door here." Ivy laughed.

"OK, baby, got to run now. Look over that program again, and I'll call when I get back in a few weeks."

"Sure, have a good trip and be safe." She very nearly added I love you but held it back. They weren't there yet.

Ivy's dryer buzzed, letting her know her load was dry. She set aside her laptop and stood to walk to the machine to fold her clothes into the basket when her phone chimed. Ivy picked it up but did not recognize the number. She thought about ignoring it but opened it and put it to her ear.

"Hello." Ivy sat back onto her faux-suede couch.

A female voice on the other end answered, "May I speak with Ivy Chandler, please?"

"This is Ivy."

"Hello, Ms. Chandler. This is Janice Strider from the Strider Agency in New York. How is your day going?"

Ivy thought she was going to faint but took a deep breath and continued. "It's going well. Do you need any more files? I thought I sent you everything you requested regarding my book series." Ivy fumbled for words.

"Oh, no, we have everything we need. Thank you for getting it to us so promptly." There was an awkward silence. Ivy suspected this was when she would hear they really weren't interested after all for some reason. "Did you have an opportunity to study our client agreement that I sent you?"

"Yes. I had an attorney friend of mine look it over, and he told me it looked to be on the up and up." Ivy bit her lip.

Did that sound like it was coming from the mouth of a stupid hick? On the up and up?

"Very good, because we'd like to offer you representation for your proposed three-book series. I've been tentatively shopping it to some publisher friends here in New York, and I'm happy to say there has been some interest. I'd like to FedEx a contract for you to sign today if that is amenable to you."

"That sounds wonderful. Thank you. Do you have my mailing address?"

"Yes, I got it from your website. I'll get this out today. I'm meeting with the acquisitions editor this afternoon from one of the Big Five, and we may just have an offer in the works for your manuscripts. How are things going in that regard? I know you have books one and two completed, but what is your projection on book three?"

"I'm about ten chapters into book three as we speak."

"Marvelous. Can you send me the first three chapters of book three? I'd love to have them to show the editor when she arrives."

"Of course. I'll send it off as soon as we hang up." Ivy saw spots before her eyes, and her heart was beating a mile a minute in her chest. *Oh, my God! Oh, my God!*

"I'll let you get to it then. Have a wonderful day, Ms. Chandler."

"You, too, and thank you." Ivy heard the line go dead, and she closed her phone. She snatched up her laptop again, logged in, and sent the requested file. Ivy went ahead and sent all ten chapters of book three, though she hadn't edited them thoroughly yet. She wanted Ms. Strider to see that she wasn't lying about her progress. After tapping the send key, Ivy slumped back on her sofa, breathless.

Is this really happening, or am I hallucinating? I have an agent and possibly a three-book deal with one of the Big Five publishers. I'm going to wake up any minute now and need coffee.

But she didn't need to wake up. She was sitting on her sofa with her laptop open and her phone on the cushion next to her. It had all really happened. Ivy thought about going to her Facebook page to announce the news but thought she'd better wait. She didn't want to jinx anything. She'd keep it all to herself until the FedEx man showed up with the contract and she'd signed it and sent it back.

She wondered if she should share the news with Carl. No, she'd wait to tell him, as well. She wasn't even certain where he was at the moment. The last word she'd had from him, he was in Milwaukee taking care of some business before going to the farm to see the kids. She hadn't heard from him in a few weeks, but that wasn't unusual when he was off on business.

9

Ivy spent the next day waiting anxiously for the doorbell to ring. When it had not by three in the afternoon, she thought about calling Ms. Strider but decided to wait. There was a three-hour time difference, and already six in the evening in New York. She resolved to call tomorrow if nobody showed up by one. It puzzled Ivy. The woman had sounded so excited the day before about getting the contract out to her that very day. Perhaps after sending the unedited beginning of the third book, she'd lost interest, or the publisher's editor had.

Ivy's stomach clenched with doubt and nerves. If she'd changed her mind, wouldn't she have at least sent an e-mail letting Ivy know? She checked her electronic mailbox for the hundredth time but found nothing from the Strider Agency.

Ivy's head pounded as she took her evening meds and crawled into bed that night, exhausted from fretting over why the contract had not arrived as promised. Ivy switched on the light and opened the newspaper. As she leafed through the pages, a familiar smiling face caught her eye. Carl, dressed in a tuxedo, stood beside a beautiful blonde in an elegant black gown, smiling up at him. Ivy's eyes flew down to the caption beneath the photo.

Real estate investor Carl Anderson and his lovely companion, Judith Merriman of the Merriman Group, attend the Arizona Realtors' Symposium, where Anderson was awarded Realtor of the Year. Last night's awards dinner was held at the Point Resort—

Last night? Ivy looked at Carl's beaming face and then that of the beautiful woman with him. Ivy put the woman in her early to mid-forties with beautiful blonde hair, ample breasts, and a slim waist. They were holding hands standing on a patio with the lights of the city shining below.

Ivy had dined at The Point, where a meal easily cost a hundred dollars a plate with wine. Jealousy surged through her, looking at the lovely woman on the page holding *her* man's hand. She couldn't understand why Carl hadn't let her know he was back in town. She looked down at the photo of Judith Merriman again. Maybe she did understand.

Look at her. I'm no competition for that. She's ten or fifteen years younger than me and has money, no doubt. I bet those rocks around her neck and wrist are real, and that dress didn't come off the rack at The Dress Barn either.

Tears streamed down Ivy's cheeks, and she pitched the paper onto the floor, the pages scattering over the carpet. The noise of the pitched pages sent Cheshire scurrying from the room. "Cowardly male," she yelled at the fleeing cat. "You're all just a bunch of damned cowards." Ivy switched off her light and sobbed into her pillows.

The combination of her nightly medication, worry from the day about the contract, and the news that Carl was back and sporting about town with a pretty young socialite got the best of Ivy. She drifted off into an exhausted but fitful sleep.

Nightmares about the Tulsa incident plagued her sleep. Judith Merriman replaced Joanna in her dreams, and rather than shielding Ivy in the planter, Carl held the elegantly dressed woman from the newspaper. Ivy woke in tears and looked at the time on the cable box by the television. The blue lights said three forty-five.

Ivy got up and trudged to the bathroom, where she relieved herself, turned on the shower, and stepped under the hot spray. It felt good, and she let the water wash away her tension from the restless night. It was a new day. Early, but a new day nonetheless. During one of her waking moments in the night, Ivy'd had an idea for her manuscript and was eager to get to it.

She made a pot of coffee, opened her laptop, and went to work on her manuscript. By noon when the rumbling of her belly told her she should eat, Ivy had finished three new chapters and almost ten thousand words.

Pleased, Ivy got up, made a sandwich, poured some root beer over ice, and returned to the couch. She considered calling New York but did not. She considered calling Carl but did not.

The doorbell rang as Ivy was taking a drink, and she choked. Coughing, she set the glass on the coffee table and went to the door. It was a Federal Express courier with a cardboard envelope. Ivy took it with a smile and signed the computer tablet. "Thank you," she said and closed the door. With shaking hands, Ivy pulled the cardboard zipper tab to open the envelope. She pulled out a stack of papers and sat down to read the cover letter from Janice Strider.

Ms. Chandler,

I'm sorry for the day's delay, but I wanted to allow my editor friend to read your additional chapters. We are both thrilled and impressed. I'm happy to inform you that her company would like to sign as your publisher for the three manuscripts and have offered the sum of three hundred thousand dollars against royalties for each book as it is submitted. They are confident, as am I, that there is a good market amongst women for your work.

Please read, sign, and date the enclosed contract. As soon as you get it back to me, I can finalize the contracts with the publisher and send you a check. I will forward you the particulars about the publishing house and what they will require from you as one of their authors.

I look forward to working with you. Janice Strider

Ivy read and reread the letter several times. Three hundred thousand dollars for *each* book? She reread it to be certain she hadn't misread it.

What if the books don't sell? Will I have to give the money back? At fifteen percent, that agency is making forty-five thousand per book. Will they have to give theirs back too? I bet not. I'd better read that contract again. They already have the first two books. Does that mean I'm going to be getting a check for a half a million dollars? Oh, my God!

Ivy took out the contract, read it, and dressed. She checked her computer for the nearest FedEx depot and drove there as quickly as she could. She had the man at the counter sign the contract as a witness to hers and had both their signatures notarized by the in-house notary. Next to buying her first house, this was the most exciting piece of business Ivy could recall. She addressed the envelope, rechecked that it was correct, and paid to have it sent off for next-day delivery.

Walking on air, Ivy returned home. She looked in her refrigerator and smiled. After getting a big check, she would be able to fill it with more than Hillshire Farms deli meat, Kraft singles, and cheap Wal-Mart root beer. Ivy wanted to dance, but dancing alone was no fun. Maybe she'd throw a party, *yes, an 'I sold my books' party*. Maybe she'd have it by the pool at The Point Resort and buy a sparkly black gown.

Ivy thought about calling Carl and sharing the good news. He had to know she'd seen the paper. She read it every day, and he knew it. He still hadn't called or texted her. At this minute, Ivy couldn't give a shit. She'd keep her happiness to herself for a little bit longer.

On second thought, she opened her laptop, logged in, and opened her Facebook page. She announced her good news about signing with the Strider Agency and the news that they'd possibly secured her a three-book deal for her latest work. After Facebook, Ivy did the same with her blog. Carl didn't have a Facebook page, and she didn't know if he followed her blog or not, but all her writing friends and fans would get the news, and that made Ivy happy at the moment.

Soon Ivy was receiving texts from friends and family members, congratulating her and asking questions about the particulars like how much money she was getting and how soon she would be getting it. Sadly, Ivy knew exactly which ones would be hitting her up for loans if she gave them details. She thanked them but refused to talk about money, saying she didn't want to jinx things.

This day was certainly better than the last. Her head swam, and she couldn't concentrate on her writing. She was happy she'd gotten up early and accomplished three chapters before the FedEx man showed.

The phone rang, and Ivy picked it up. It was not a number she recognized, but it wasn't a New York area code either. She opened the phone.

"Hello, Ivy Chandler here," she chirped.

"Miss Chandler, this is Norman Powell from Branson. I showed you and Mr. Anderson some properties a while back." Ivy recognized his nasally Southern accent now.

"Yes, Mr. Powell, what can I do for you?" Ivy couldn't remember giving him one of her cards, but she must have.

"I've been tryin' to reach Mr. Anderson. We have a date set for the closin' on the condos, but I wanted to let him know that the little cabin I showed y'all is available again. I thought twice that we had it sold when he made an offer on it, but those deals fell through, and it's available again." Powell paused and coughed. "Do you happen to have another number where I might reach him?"

"No, I'm sorry. His cell is the only phone he has. He's been traveling, but I think he may be home now. If you leave a message, I'm sure he'll return your call."

"Thank you, ma'am. I've been leavin' him messages for a few days now, and I haven't heard from him. If you happen to talk to him, will you let him know the cabin is available again and his offer of one fifty could still be presented to the owner? After this last deal fell through, I believe the seller might be open to it. If not, I'll be seein' Mr. Anderson at the closin' on the condos in two weeks. Will you be accompanyin' him?"

"I don't think so, Mr. Powell. Mr. Anderson

doesn't generally take me on his business trips. We were together there because the Tulsa conference was canceled, and we thought we'd run up to Branson for a little working vacation." Ivy sighed, thinking of the quaint little cabin. "If I talk to him, I'll be sure to let him know about the cabin."

"Thank you, and you have a nice day, ma'am." He hung up, and Ivy closed her phone.

Should I call him? Was he going to buy that cabin for me? For us?

Confused, Ivy picked up the phone and punched in Carl's number. It rang several times before going to voicemail. Ivy hung up. She would not leave a message for him on voicemail. He'd recognize her number and return her call, or he wouldn't.

10

Carl did not call. Ivy scanned the paper every day but found no more pictures of him with Judith Merriman. Ivy had googled her and found that the woman was forty-six, twice divorced, and the mother of two sons. Since the death of her father, Howard Merriman, two years ago, she'd returned to using her maiden name and headed the Merriman Group, a real estate investment firm that owned several shopping malls in the valley, Tucson, and Flagstaff. To say the woman was rich would be a gross understatement.

There's no way I can compete with that. She's younger. She's beautiful. She's rich, and she knows his business better than I ever will. What do I have to offer compared to her? She probably puts out, too.

Ten days after returning the contract to Janice Strider, the FedEx man was back at her door with another envelope. Ivy sat in stunned disbelief staring at a check for five hundred and ten thousand dollars. Her stomach lurched, and she hardly had time to grab the metal wastebasket next to the couch before she emptied her stomach. Ivy sat shaking for several minutes then threw up again, staring at the large check on the cushion beside her.

What am I going to do with this kind of money? Does half a million count as rich or just wealthy? No, just damned lucky is what it is.

Ivy tucked the check carefully into her wallet. She changed into jeans, a tank top, and a light linen jacket. She brushed her hair and stared at her reflection in the mirror. She needed a haircut. She could certainly afford one now. Ivy picked up her wallet and went out to her car. She looked at the dusty old sedan. She needed a new car, too. Ivy clutched her wallet, holding the ridiculously large check. She could afford one of those now, too.

Don't go getting carried away and spend it all in one day, Iva Leigh. That's what Granny would say if she were here to hear about this good fortune.

Ivy drove to the bank, where she put half the money into a high-interest money market account, paid off her credit card, and raised the limit from the prepaid five hundred to five thousand. The rest she deposited into her regular savings account, less five hundred in cash that she put into her wallet for spending money.

After getting her car washed and detailed, Ivy went to a salon and got herself detailed. She got a new haircut, fresh color, her nails done, and her brows waxed. She'd never felt so pampered in her life. She spent over two hundred dollars at the salon and didn't feel bad about it one little bit. She deserved a little special treatment after all her hard work on her manuscripts. Writing wasn't backbreaking, but it still amounted to work of the mental variety.

The next day Ivy picked up her sister, and they went shopping. Carrie was thrilled for her but warned her to be careful with the money and not go crazy with her spending. When Ivy pulled into a luxury car dealership, Carrie just rolled her eyes and shook her head in resignation. When they drove out of the dealership in a sporty new electric-blue Lexus sedan that was paid for free and clear, they both wore broad smiles on their faces.

Ivy drove the new car to Scottsdale, where they visited some high-end consignment shops Carrie knew about, and then stopped for lunch at a nice restaurant. From outside, Ivy could smell fragrant wood-smoke from a meat smoker, and her mouth began to water. Her mood darkened when she walked past Carl's silver Lexus in the parking lot. Ivy recognized the plates. Inside the restaurant, the rooms were decorated with Southwestern furniture and art. Navajo rugs hung on the wall, and the head of an elk hung over the massive fireplace.

The hostess seated them, and Ivy looked around the room to see Carl sitting next to Judith Merriman in a booth up the aisle from her table. She swallowed hard and tried to look away, but she could not.

As she and Carrie were ordering, Carl finally noticed her and gave her a little nervous smile and nod. Ivy didn't think the chattering Judith had noticed. When she and Carl stood, Ivy saw two young men had been sitting with them on the other side of the booth. They must be Judith's two boys. They both had their mother's blond hair and delicate features.

Carl gave Ivy a slight nod as he walked by but did not speak. Ivy wanted to weep but kept smiling and joking with Carrie. Her phone chirped, notifying her of a text, and Ivy opened it. The text came from Carl.

Hi baby. Will call you later.

Ivy replied, *Don't bother.* She snapped the phone off and shoved it back into her pocket.

"Who was that? Carrie asked.

"Nobody important. Where do you want to go after lunch?"

"I think we should go look at apartments." She took a bite of her salad. "You don't like that place you're in now. Find yourself something nicer."

"I'm going to stay where I am for a while. I think I might travel for a bit."

"You're gonna put miles on that new car and drop the value," Carrie warned. "You need to stay in one place until you get that last book finished. How much more do you have to go until it's done?"

"I'm about halfway there. The other two are thirty chapters each, and I have fifteen finished on this one." Ivy stabbed at a piece of chicken in her spinach salad, still upset about seeing Carl with that woman and her sons. He'd avoided every effort Ivy had made to get him to meet her family, but here he was out having a cheerful lunch with Judith's.

"Then you'd better quit spending money until you get it finished," Carrie chided.

"OK, Granny, then. I guess you're paying for lunch?" Ivy pushed the check toward her sister.

Carrie opened it, and her eyes went wide. "Nope, you're paying this one." She laughed and pushed the bill back to Ivy.

They finished their lunch and stopped at the mall, where Ivy bought some new jeans, a dressy linen suit, a new purse, and shoes. She saw Carrie eying a specific designer purse, and while Carrie wasn't looking, Ivy picked it up along with the matching wallet. She had the cashier bag them separated from hers and handed them to Carrie when they got to the car.

"What's this?" Carrie asked as Ivy loaded her purchases into the back of her new car.

"Look and see." Ivy watched her sister's face brighten when she saw the designer bag and wallet.

"Iva Leigh, what did you do that for?"

"I bought my sister a present. Lord knows she's bought me enough over the past few years."

Carrie hugged her, clutching the bag in her hand. "Thanks, Sis. I love it." She got into the car. "Now stop spending all your money until you get that next book finished."

"Yes, Granny." Ivy laughed and got behind the wheel.

She dropped Carrie off without going in and drove back toward her apartment. Her phone rang, and she answered without looking at the caller ID.

"Hello, Ivy Chandler here."

"Miss Chandler, this is Norm Powell from Branson again. Have you, by chance, spoken with Mr. Anderson?" He sounded worried. "He hasn't returned my calls, and the seller of that cabin is getting anxious. Mr. Anderson is supposed to be here next week for that closin', but I thought if I could make the offer, we could do all of them at one time."

"Mr. Powell, why don't you present that offer to the seller in my name?" Ivy said boldly. "I liked that place, and if Carl is dragging his feet on it, I'll take it."

"At what price?" Powell asked.

"One fifty, just like Mr. Anderson offered," Ivy said curtly, knowing the realtor was hoping for a higher offer.

"I can make the offer, Miss Chandler, but I can't guarantee the owner will take it. The last offer was two twenty-five."

"Mr. Powell, you told me last week the seller was

motivated and would probably take one-fifty," Ivy said sternly. "I have cash if that helps. I can wire you earnest money if you need it before making the offer."

"Do you have a fax number where I can send you the proposal offer? I'd need ten percent down with the offer to go into escrow against the sales price."

Ivy gave him her fax number. "Can you text me the routing information so I can go by my bank and send the funds?"

"Yes, ma'am, I most certainly can, but how long would it take you to get over to your bank? I'm just outside mine now and could wait here and fax the agreement directly to your bank." Ivy heard him take a deep breath. "We could just take care of the whole thing right there. I'll call the seller in the meantime and make him the offer. I should know something by the time you get to your bank."

"I'll be there in about fifteen minutes, Mr. Powell. I'm in my car now." She gave him the name and address of her bank so his banker could make the necessary connections with hers. Rather than going back to her apartment, Ivy made yet another trip to her bank. It would be her third and, she hoped, the final one for the day.

When Ivy walked into the bank, it was early afternoon but not nearly closing time. For their newest large depositor, the manager was more than happy to assist her with her business. He already had the faxed sales agreement from Mr. Powell and only needed her to sign a receipt for the funds to be released to the escrow account at Mr. Powell's bank in Branson.

"The seller," Mr. Powell told her as she walked up the stairs into the bank, "is willing to take the one fifty so long as it's a quick cash deal and we don't have to do any inspections or surveys. He'd like to close as soon as humanly possible."

"Would three days from now be quick enough?" Ivy asked as she shook the bank manager's hand.

"What?" Powell asked in a shocked voice on the other end of the phone. "Yes, yes, of course, that would be most accommodating indeed. Can you get here in three days? Why don't we make it four just to be on the safe side? The seller is also out of state and will have to get here, as well."

"That's fine," Ivy told him, "I'll have my banker transfer the funds into your escrow account today, and I'll see you at your office in four days at nine-thirty in the morning."

"You're havin' all the funds wired today?" he asked, shocked.

"I'd really rather not travel with that kind of money on me. Your escrow company will hold it until closing, will it not?"

"It most certainly will, Miss Chandler. You need not worry about improprieties on my end."

"Of course not, Mr. Powell. Consider it done, and I'll see you in four days to sign the papers and pick up the keys."

Ivy signed and initialed the sales offer agreement, signed the release of funds from her account, and waited for the receipt from Powell's escrow account. She drove home over two hundred thousand dollars lighter than when she'd left.

Ivy called Carrie and asked her to please come over and tend to Cheshire again while she was out of town but skipped over the details. Ivy told her sister she was going back to Branson to finish up some business she and Carl had started there. Carrie didn't pry, though Ivy knew she wanted to know exactly what was really going on.

Back at home, Ivy cuddled with Cheshire then began packing for yet another trip. It would give her a chance to see what sort of mileage the new car got on the highway. Ivy packed her new jeans, some blouses, and the linen suit with matching shoes.

She didn't plan on staying longer than it would take to get the papers signed and the utilities connected at the cabin. This would be a quick trip, and then she would have to make plans to move everything. Ivy found the thought of living somewhere green again inviting. There would be four seasons with spring flowers, summer rainstorms, fall colors, and maybe even snow at Christmas. She would be closer to two of her children and grandchildren.

These were things Ivy had put on the plus column when trying to make her decision about moving to the Ozarks with Carl. Now she sat planning to move without him, and it was breaking her heart.

11

Ivy snuggled with Cheshire, made sure his litter box was clean and his dishes full. She put down two extras of each in case her sister didn't get over promptly.

The sun hadn't risen as Ivy loaded her cheap cloth suitcases into the trunk of her new luxury automobile. It had been a long time since she'd owned a brand new car, and it cheered her that this one didn't come with payments. Calling her insurance agent the day before, Ivy had made the changes for coverage on the Lexus. She cruised up the I-17, filled with wonder and excitement. She was heading out on a new adventure and possibly the beginning of the best part of her life.

Who knew, if these books sold well, maybe there would be other big paychecks in her future. Ivy had already started planning another book set in the Old West. She would have to do a little more research but thought she might put the story in Missouri when that state was the West. That would set it well before the Civil War.

Ivy loved doing the research, and now that her home would be in Missouri, she would have easy access to libraries, university archives, and museums, as well as some of the old buildings in the actual towns she might feature. New projects, like new adventures, excited her.

As Ivy transferred from the I-17 to the I-40, her phone rang. She answered it.

"Hello, Ivy Chandler here, how may I help you?"

"You always sound so professional, baby." It was Carl, and Ivy very nearly disconnected her phone.

"Hi, Carl. What's up?" Ivy didn't want to sound curt or unpleasant, but she found it challenging.

"I just wanted to talk to you about at the restaurant yesterday." Had it really only been yesterday? So much had happened it seemed to Ivy like weeks had passed since watching Carl laughing and eating with Judith Merriman and her sons.

"What about it?" Ivy asked, wanting to pitch the phone over her shoulder into the back seat. "When did you get back into town?" Ivy wondered if he'd tell her the truth.

"I've been back a little over a week. I had to come back for a conference here I'd completely forgotten about." Well, partially true.

"I'm sorry I didn't call. I've been a little tied up with things since I got back into town."

"I could see that." Ivy huffed and lowered the visor to shade her eyes from the early morning sun rising ahead of her.

"Now, baby, you know we never had any strings on one another. We're both free spirits and play the field. Judith is an old friend, and she's been having some trouble with one of her boys. Their dad's not in the picture any longer, and she thought maybe I could help. I've been making myself available and spending some time with her and the kids."

"How very thoughtful of you," Ivy sneered.

"So how have you been, baby? How's it going with the writing?" he asked in a lighthearted tone, purposely ignoring hers. Ivy could tell he was eager to change the subject away from Judith Merriman.

"Pretty good, actually, I'm half finished with book three."

"No news from that agent yet?" he asked sympathetically.

"Actually, they signed me."

"That's great, baby. Maybe you'll be in the big bucks soon," he chuckled.

"I already am. I was out with my sister yesterday, celebrating my three-book deal at three hundred K a pop. I got the check for the first two books the day before yesterday." It still stunned her that it had been only two days ago.

"That's awesome, Ivy. I'm so proud of you." He paused, but Ivy didn't respond. "Shall we go out and celebrate tonight? You can buy since you're flush with cash."

"I can't. I'm not home. I'm taking my new car out for a spin. I'll be gone for a week or two, I think."

"Cash burning a hole in your pocket?" He chuckled.

"I guess, but my old girl was on her last legs, and I liked your Lexus so much I bought one for myself. I'm taking it on a road trip to see how it shakes out."

"That's great, baby, but be careful how you spend your money. You may need it to last."

"Now you sound like my sister," Ivy huffed, irritated with him even further. "Neither of you think I have any more books in me." Her phone beeped, letting her know she had a text coming in. "I gotta go now, Carl. I have another call coming in."

"OK, baby. I guess you're in the big leagues now and in demand. Be careful, and I'll call you later."

Carl hung up before she could say goodbye. Ivy plugged her phone into the charger. She would check her text when she stopped for fuel. It was probably her sister texting good morning.

Ivy came to a truck stop about a hundred miles before the New Mexico border and stopped. The car wasn't near empty, but she wasn't familiar with this vehicle yet and didn't want to get stuck in the middle of nowhere without any gas.

Carl did call her later, and they talked for over an hour as she crossed New Mexico. He talked around the subject but never mentioned the Branson deal. She didn't mention *her* Branson deal either.

Powell had called Carl and left him messages. If he'd wanted to go forward on the cabin deal, he would have responded. The way Ivy saw it, Carl Anderson had lost out, and his loss was her gain.

Maybe he planned to move Judith into one of the condos on the lake or into one of the fancier log houses they'd looked at. Judith Merriman didn't look to Ivy to be the little country cabin type and would be a much better real estate partner than Ivy Chandler. She was probably better in the sack as well. Carl liked his women with long hair, big boobs, and long legs. Judith had all of those and a big real estate company worth millions to go along with it. Ivy Chandler, even with her newfound luck, could not compete with that. She wasn't even sure she wanted to any longer.

Ivy tried to push the thought of Carl and the beautiful, leggy blonde together naked in a shower out of her mind's eye, but she found it challenging. He hadn't mentioned her again during their conversation. When Ivy had asked him about his granddaughter's birthday, he'd told her he'd had to miss it because of coming back to the valley for the forgotten conference.

Ivy never mentioned seeing the photo in the paper, and neither did he. She wanted so badly to bring it up, but Ivy held her tongue, hoping Carl would come forward with the information. He didn't, and it hurt Ivy's feelings. It also shattered her confidence in there being any future with Carl Anderson.

He was correct. They had no real commitment to one another. They were not exclusive, and Ivy had been out on dates with other men when Carl was traveling. She'd always been open with him about those dates, however, and had never tried to hide them from him.

Ivy stopped for dinner at The Big Texan in Amarillo and watched some fool try to eat the seventy-two-ounce steak dinner. He couldn't do it and ended up puking what he'd stuffed down his throat into a bucket. Ivy enjoyed her rare rib-eye with all the trimmings.

When she finished her meal, she very nearly checked into the adjoining motel. Her day had started early, and she was tired now that her belly was full, but she decided to push on and try to get a little closer to Oklahoma City. Ivy filled the tank of the Lexus with premium fuel and made her way back onto the eastbound I-40.

As the sun fell behind her, lightning flashed in the sky ahead. If it began to rain, Ivy would find a hotel. She did not like to drive in the dark, especially in the rain. At her last fuel stop, Ivy had purchased a James Patterson mystery audiobook. She popped in the next CD and listened to the riveting tale as she drove. About an hour west of Oklahoma City, heavy rain began to fall. Ivy pulled off the highway and checked into a Knight's Inn.

The room was typical highway chic, smelling musty, of stale cigarette smoke and Pine-Sol. Ivy flipped on the television in time to catch a tornado warning. She shook her head, showered, and crawled into bed. Thunder boomed and rattled the pane of the big window hidden behind the heavy blackout curtains. Ivy got up and peeked out the drapes to see rain pelting the pavement and glowing in the halogen lights around the parking lot. Ivy worried about her car, hoping there would be no hail associated with this storm. Fearing she would be rousted from her bed to be herded to a storm shelter, Ivy pulled on her long sleepshirt before crawling back between the soft, cool sheets.

She left the television on and was jarred awake twice by the blaring of the National Weather Service warnings. Ivy jumped up both times to look out the window. It still rained, and the trees in the distance danced in the winds, but nothing that kept her from drifting back to sleep.

Ivy and her siblings had grown up in Tornado Alley in the Midwest, and unless the shingles were being peeled off the roof or tree limbs were falling from the sky, she didn't get flustered by a thunderstorm. Even after her experience in Tulsa, Ivy let the rhythm of the storm lull her back to sleep.

She actually missed them. They did not get many thunderstorms in Phoenix. During the summer monsoons, storms came up from the South and plagued the southeast valley. In the winter months, the storms came in from California and drenched the west valley. Ivy's apartment, situated in north-central Phoenix, rarely saw any rough weather in either season.

Morning dawned with drizzle but no thunder or lightning. The wind had calmed, and Ivy drove away toward Oklahoma City at half-past seven. She found a drive-thru at a nearby McDonald's and got a large black coffee, a sausage and egg muffin, and a hash brown.

Ivy plugged her phone into the dashboard charger, put in another audiobook CD, and headed back down I-40. The clouds and drizzle obscured the morning sun, so the drive wasn't too uncomfortable.

The Lexus handled nicely on the wet pavement, and Ivy had become accustomed to the brakes and the cruise control system. She was still figuring out the radio, lights, and air conditioning controls. Those would come with time and experience.

The traffic in Oklahoma City was trying, with all the road construction, and Ivy found herself idling for long stretches. She was happy when the transition onto the I-44 tollway came into view, heading her toward Tulsa and then on to Branson. Ivy thought she should make it into town before dark if the weather continued to hold.

Her Patterson novel ended, and Ivy checked her fuel gauge. She still had half a tank, but Ivy thought she'd stop at the next truck stop for a fill-up and another audiobook. It was near to lunch-time, so she'd probably pick up a sandwich as well.

No large truck stops appeared for over an hour along the state-run tollway. When one finally came up, there weren't many cars in front or at the pumps. Ivy pulled in, filled her tank, and pulled the car up to the front of the big store. After filling the tank of the Lexus, she went in and emptied hers, using the sterile tiled restroom before venturing into the store itself.

The aroma of sandwiches coming from the Subway caught Ivy's attention, and she made that her next stop. She ordered a turkey with bacon on an Italian roll with sweet onion dressing, chose a bag of chips, and filled a waxed cardboard cup with root beer. Ivy picked up the tray and slid into one of the smooth Formica booths.

Only one other person sat in the restaurant area, a big, middle-aged man wearing a ball cap emblazoned with a sports logo Ivy didn't recognize and a grease-stained t-shirt that bulged over his muscular shoulders and upper arms. Ivy suspected him of being a truck driver. He smiled at her, flashing even, white teeth, and she smiled back nervously. He rose, and Ivy admired the way his jeans clung tightly to his shapely behind. He piled his garbage onto his tray and walked away past her booth.

Ivy opened her chips, poured them onto the paper that had wrapped her sandwich, and took a long drink of the icy root beer through the clear plastic straw. She was biting into her sandwich when someone slid into her booth on the other side of the table. Ivy looked up to see the same man who'd been at the other table.

"Hi," he said with a blinding smile and dazzling hazel eyes. "I'm Dan, and I just had to come back and tell you I think you're the most beautiful woman I've seen in days."

Ivy swallowed her bite of sandwich and washed it down with some more soda. "Thanks," she said with an impish smile. "Does that line get you much action out here on the road?"

"Some." He picked up one of her chips and popped it into his mouth. "Pretty and smart, too. I like that. Where are ya headed?"

"Branson. You?" Ivy took another bite of her tasty sandwich.

"I'm running a load of produce from Brawley, California, to St. Louis." He picked up another of her chips and then boldly took a drink from her root beer. "You're not one of those Osmond Brothers fans, are you?" he asked, smiling as he chewed.

"Hardly." Ivy chuckled. "I just bought some property near there. I'll live there part-time, and my sons and grandchildren will use it during the summers and hunting season."

"Huh. Why part-time? Where will you be living for the rest of the time?" He flashed his charming smile again, and he was beginning to make Ivy a little nervous. He seemed just a bit too charming.

"I live in Phoenix. You?" Ivy snatched a chip before Dan could take another.

"Victorville, California. I'm a desert rat too now." He took another drink from her straw. "If you're headed to Branson, we could travel together for a bit. You have ears in your wheels?"

"No," Ivy laughed, "I gave up my CB thirty years ago. I traded it in for audiobooks." She wadded the paper from her sandwich into a ball, piled her trash onto the tray, and stood. "It's why I stopped. I need a fresh one." Ivy walked to the can and dumped the trash. She took one last drink and dropped the cup to join the rest of the garbage.

"What do you like to listen to?" he asked as he followed her to the audiobook section. "I like the Deathlands stories and action thrillers."

"Sex and violence," Ivy said as she browsed, "got ya." She picked up a Clive Cussler title and turned to walk back toward the checkout counter. "I just finished a pretty good James Patterson if you'd like it," Ivy offered. "I just pass them along when I'm finished."

"Like I said, pretty and smart." He stood back, watching as Ivy paid for her purchase with her Mastercard. She picked up the plastic bag and walked toward the glass doors. Dan followed behind. Ivy got out the door and pushed the button on the key fob to unlock and start the bright blue Lexus.

"Nice ride." Dan opened the door for her, and Ivy slipped in. She picked up the CD case for the James Patterson novel from the white leather passenger's seat and handed it to Dan.

"Here you go. Enjoy."

"Thanks, but what I'd really enjoy is you driving back by my rig and climbing up so I could show you my very comfy sleeper-cab." He ran a firm hand over her hair and grinned lasciviously down at Ivy.

"I have someplace I have to be." Ivy twisted her neatly bobbed brunette head out of his grasp, smiling into his pretty eyes. "Thanks for the offer, but I really have to get going."

"You have a card or something with your number so I can call the next time I'm through Phoenix? I think I'd like to get to know you better."

Eager to be shed of the man, Ivy dug into the outside pocket of her wallet for a business card and handed it to him. "I'm going to be away for a while, but I have my phone with me all the time."

He studied her business card before tucking it into his back pocket. Ivy noticed the wedding ring on the man's left hand and gave a sad mental sigh. "Well, nice to have met you, Ivy Chandler. Do you think I've ever read anything you've written?"

"I seriously doubt it. I write women's historical fiction. You know, stories about the plight of women during the Civil War or traveling across the prairie, fighting off desperados and wild Indians. I don't write post-apocalyptic claptrap or action thrillers that appeal to most men."

"I'll look for your stuff the next time I'm in Barnes and Noble." He doffed his cap, turned, and walked back into the air-conditioned store. Ivy wanted to tell him not to bother looking in Barnes and Noble, but she didn't because one day soon, her books would be featured there. She smiled, shut the door, popped in the first CD of the new audiobook, and made her way back to the highway.

Ivy passed through Tulsa and saw how many trees still showed signs of the violence wrought by the storm the month before. Orange trucks and crews dressed in the same color labored at stringing new power lines. Ivy wondered why the power companies didn't bury all their lines underground here, where significant storms ripped apart lines every year. She looked at the orange-clad men and wondered if it weren't simply a way to keep folks in the area employed.

Passing through patches of drizzle and hard rain between Tulsa and Branson slowed Ivy's travel, but she checked into the Best Western just after ten that night. Much more posh than the Howard Johnson — Ivy wondered why Carl had chosen the older hotel for their vacation rather than this nicer Best Western. She remembered her mother's comment about how rich men hung onto their money. Ivy looked at the receipt in her hand and knew she would not be rich long if she stayed in nice hotels rather than the more practical cheaper ones.

Ivy undressed, showered, and slipped into her sleep shirt. She turned on the television and found the Discovery ID channel. The drone of the narrators and the lack of loud musical commercials supplied white noise that drowned out the ringing in her ears from tinnitus and allowed her to sleep.

12

Norman Powell didn't expect her until the next morning, so Ivy took the opportunity to explore. Dressed casually in jeans and a t-shirt, she found a hole-in-the-wall diner and had some greasy eggs, bacon, and pancakes for breakfast. The young waitress was good, keeping the coffee cup topped off. She left the busy girl a five-dollar tip for a six-dollar breakfast.

Ivy had spent the first ten years of her working life waitressing. She appreciated good service and rewarded it. When she got poor service, she might leave a penny or a nickel to emphasize her displeasure.

The weather was sunny and warm but not overly hot, considering the season. The humidity was higher than Ivy was accustomed to in Phoenix, but this wasn't bad at all, compared to what she'd endured as a child in their old farmhouse without air conditioning. A gentle breeze blew, and the overhanging limbs of massive oaks, maples, and sycamores shaded the narrow country roads around Branson. Ivy avoided the main street, still jammed with tourists as the summer season hadn't ended and many children hadn't yet started back to school. Ivy suspected that after the Labor Day weekend, this place would dry up and be much easier to traverse.

The music halls would continue to attract people on the weekends, and hunting seasons like deer, turkey, and wild hog would attract visitors, as well as duck and goose hunters and the constant hordes of fishermen visiting Lake of the Ozarks.

Ivy made several wrong turns before she finally found the road leading to her cabin. It made her happy to see a red 'sold' placard draped across the real estate sign in the yard. Ivy turned into the gravel drive to find it muddy from the recent heavy rains in the area.

The yard had been mowed but not raked, and thick rows of brown grass crossed the yard. Adding a yard rake to her mental list of necessities, Ivy got out of the car and walked around the cabin a few times before stepping up onto the shady porch. She sat down in the porch swing and enjoyed the breeze blowing from across the field beyond the cabin.

Ivy wondered about the people who'd lived here before. Had they been a couple? Did they have children? What sort of life had they lived here? Ivy could see signs of a large garden out back, and the remains of dead flowering plants lined the walkway and the front of the long porch.

Hedge roses lined the edges of the property to the east and west. Ivy closed her eyes and imagined sitting here with her laptop on her knees, writing with the scent of roses and fresh-cut grass in her nose.

Living here would be a joy, and there was room for her family to visit. She thought she would put a set of twin beds in the second bedroom and find a nice pull-out sofa for the living room. Ivy thought back on Carl's expensive antiques. She made another mental note to look up antique malls in the area and make a list of everything she might want or need. For the first time in her life, Ivy could walk into a store and not worry about not having enough money to buy whatever she might like to have. She smiled with satisfaction to herself.

Ivy readjusted her behind on the wooden swing. The next thing going on her list would be a thick cushion for this swing. She intended to be spending a good bit of time out here and wanted to be comfortable. Ivy took a deep breath of the clean, damp air. This place had so much potential, and she planned to make it her own, filled with country antiques and comfortable furniture. She would inquire of Mr. Powell about furniture stores and the like in the area after the closing tomorrow.

An old pickup passed, slowed to a stop, and began backing up. A woman about Ivy's age pulled into the mouth of the drive and got out. Her short, curly hair was salt-and-peppered. She wore jeans, a sloppy t-shirt covered with a loose plaid cotton shirt, and white leather tennis shoes.

"Hi there. You the person buying this place?" She walked with a steady purpose to join Ivy on the porch. She extended her rough hand. "Peggy Martin. My husband and I own the place just up the road from here." She pointed toward the west where Ivy could see the blue shingled roof of a house beyond the trees lining the road.

Ivy grasped the woman's extended hand. "Ivy Chandler, and yes, I just bought this place."

"It's a good place. My cousin Cindy and her husband built it about twenty years ago. Her husband put it up for sale after she passed from cancer last year."

Ivy sat and motioned for Peggy to join her. "I'm sorry for your loss. What can you tell me about the place?"

"You plannin' to live here, or are you gonna use it as a seasonal rental? Cindy would have liked to see a regular resident over drunken hunters and college kids partyin' and cuttin' up. Her husband's moved away now and could care less so long as he gets the money from the sale to pay off his silly truck."

"I'm going to be living here most of the time. I have a place in Phoenix, so I might go back there for the winters. I haven't decided yet."

"That's nice. Me and my husband have been on that farm all our lives. He was born there and inherited it from his daddy when the old man passed. I was seventeen when we married and moved in there with him and his parents." She shook her head and rubbed her hands on her thighs. "You married, or are you gonna be livin' here by your lonesome?"

"I'm single. I tried marriage three times, but it didn't agree with me." Ivy chuckled. "I have three children, and my sons will more than likely visit here from Indiana during hunting seasons or to fish. The grandkids like to go tubing too."

"That's big doins' 'round here." She stood. "Well, welcome to the neighborhood, Ivy, nice to meet you. Do you attend church? We belong to the Oak Glen Baptist Church if you'd care to join us on Sundays."

"I'm probably going to be busy getting settled in here for a while, and I'm not much of a churchgoer, but thanks for the offer." Ivy watched the woman's face darken. "Peggy, could you recommend a furniture store and an antique mall in the area? I need to furnish this place."

"Most new folks drive into Springfield for new furniture, but Mayer's is the local furniture store most of us buy from. There are a bunch of antique stores around. That place up on Route 10 is pretty popular. Cindy did a lot of her shopping there. I think they call it Found Again or some such nonsense. It's just a bunch of over-priced used junk our parents and grandparents threw out years ago." She laughed uneasily.

"Thanks, Peggy, I'll check them out."

"Most of us do our grocery shopping at the IGA in town, but lots of folks are using the Wal-Mart now that they expanded and added a grocery section. There's a farmers' market downtown on Fridays, too."

"That's great. I'll go down to the farmers' market for sure." That made Peggy smile.

"They soak us for the space rent, but it's a good way to get rid of produce we can't put up."

"I noticed there's a big garden spot and a greenhouse out back."

"Cindy had a real green thumb," Peggy said with a sad smile, nodding. "That woman would take the seedlings the feed store was going to throw out and nurse them back into the healthiest plants you'd ever want to see. She had a chicken coop back there, too, but *he* sold it and the chickens right after Cindy passed." She sighed. "Cindy loved those damned birds, and the fresh eggs were great. She'd bring the extras up to the market sometimes." Peggy walked back, climbed into her pickup, and backed out of the drive, waving.

After watching the old pickup disappear around the wooded bend, Ivy walked to the back of the cabin and found the thin spot in the grass where the chicken coop must have stood. Holes pocked the ground where fence posts set in concrete had been dug out. It had been a big coop. Ivy remembered gathering fresh eggs on their farm in Indiana as a child. Maybe a chicken coop would be nice. She'd have to check out the local feed store or farm supply outlet. Ivy wondered if she'd be able to remember all of this later without writing it down.

As Ivy drove back to town, it began to drizzle. Ivy flipped on the windshield wipers and drove back toward the hotel. When a sign at the side of the blacktop marked the turnoff to Route 10, she took it. About six miles up the road, a giant metal building with a sign announced the Found Again Antique Mall. Ivy looked at the clock on the dash. It read one fifteen. The store should surely be open. She saw only three vehicles in the parking lot and parked next to a panel van with the store's logo on the side. Ivy got out and walked inside the huge metal building. A withered, balding old man greeted her at the counter.

"Good afternoon, miss. How may I assist you today?" He smiled at her with yellowed teeth and the watery eyes of advanced years.

"Hi," Ivy greeted in return, "I just bought a cabin here, and I need to furnish it." Ivy looked around the building stuffed to the rafters with antiques and other discarded household items. The store was heavenly, but shopping alone was no fun. She wished Carl was here with her. He had an eye for quality, and Ivy was certain they could happily spend hours together in a place like this.

"I'm Humphry. Are you looking to furnish any room in particular?"

"I need to furnish them all." Ivy laughed. "I need a dining table, living room things, and stuff for two bedrooms."

"Are you planning to decorate in any particular style?"

"Country chic to nineteenth-century Victorian."

"Which cabin did you buy? There have been several on the market lately," the old man asked as he walked from around the counter, sensing a large sale coming his way.

"The two-bedroom on County Road 410 East." Ivy admired a purple etched-glass hurricane lamp that had been converted from oil to electrical use. She looked at the tag that read eighty-five dollars. "I'll take this," Ivy said, knowing the price was fair if the electrical conversion actually worked.

"That's Cindy Wingate's place, isn't it?" He picked up the fragile but heavy glass lamp and walked it carefully to the counter. "Cindy was one of my best customers. Her husband hated antiques, but he loved that woman, God rest her sweet soul, and let her have whatever she wanted. Is that converted cook stove still in her kitchen?

"Her husband sold most of her things, but she'd come back and haunt him if he took that out of the house. Cindy spent a fortune refinishing and refitting that stove to work in the kitchen of that cabin. It looked outstanding when she was done with it, too."

"It's still there, and it looks absolutely perfect," Ivy told him as they walked back to a section that was kitchen and dining room items. He led her to a round oak pedestal table with four rounded-back Windsor chairs. Ivy looked around at the other items on display in the area.

She went directly to an oak pie safe with a row of small drawers under the doors, screened with chicken wire rather than glassed. She pulled on a ceramic knob below the top of the counter and was pleased to find the original galvanized flour bin still intact. Ivy's mother had one just like it that she'd found at a yard sale. It had been painted blue, and

Ivy remembered her mother laboring for hours scraping off layer after layer of other colors of paint until she got down to the honey-gold oak beneath.

Ivy looked at the tag that read two hundred and seventy-five dollars. The tag on one of the oak chairs told her the five pieces were five hundred and fifty.

"I'll take the dining set and the pie safe," Ivy told the beaming old man.

"Cindy would have loved all these pieces," he told her as he took out a red pen and marked the tags as sold.

They walked up some other aisles until they came to a collection of bedroom furniture. A tall wardrobe caught Ivy's eye. Someone had painted it white to give it a shabby chic look with bouquets of pastel roses stenciled onto the ovals carved into the tall doors. She opened it. They'd painted the inside white as well and fitted tall mirrors securely to the inside of the doors. Ivy rolled her eyes at the four hundred dollar price tag, but she didn't disregard the lovely piece completely. The man had packed the area with shabby chic items, and Ivy could see a room decked out with it and trimmed with cabbage roses in shades of pink.

"Isn't painting this stuff supposed to lower the value of antiques?" Ivy asked Humphry, who was reorganizing glassware upon the top of a bureau with an ornately carved mirror. The redesigner had painted the roses carved into the frame various shades of pink and the foliage around them soft greens.

"If it isn't oak or mahogany, the value doesn't really decrease much, and this shabby chic stuff appeals to the Yuppies who watch those decorating shows on HGTV," he said and laughed.

Ivy hated to admit it, but it appealed to her, as well. There was just something girly about it.

"What size is this bed?" Ivy asked about a brightly polished brass headboard and footboard propped against a wall.

"It's not an antique," Humphry admitted, "and I think it's a queen. I had it set up here because it looks good with the white stuff."

Ivy bit her lip and looked around. "Humphry, give me a price on all of this." She swept her hand around the display to include the wardrobe, the bureau with its painted mirror, two nightstands, a rocking chair, and the brass bed. "I want the topiaries on that bureau and the pink chenille bedspread draped over the rocker, as well."

"Oh, my goodness. You're going to make my week, young lady." He gave her a price of eight hundred, but Ivy talked him down to six since she would still have to buy a mattress and box spring for the bed.

By the time Ivy slid her Mastercard, she had furniture for every room and had accumulated a bill of nearly two thousand dollars. She'd found a set of oak twin beds, a nightstand and a tall dresser for the guest room, a coffee table and end tables for the living room, a beautiful set of china complete with a tea service, several Victorian lamps, and a giant deer head with shiny brown glass eyes to mount over the fireplace.

Every proper nineteenth-century home had a dead thing hanging on the wall or mounted on a table someplace. A sturdy set of wicker furniture rounded out her purchases, and it would look beautiful set up on the opposite end of the porch from the swing, and matching cushions would coordinate it all.

A trip into town to find a nice sleeper sofa along with mattresses would be her final furniture purchase for the time being. Carrie would have a fit about her spending so much money, but she had to have furniture. Humphry had also given her the name and address of a local woman who made braided woven rugs. Those would be perfect to finish the look Ivy hoped to achieve.

13

Ivy arrived at Norman Powell's office promptly at nine-thirty. He didn't arrive until nine-forty-five. His secretary apologized and took her into a small room with a round table, chairs, and a water cooler.

"Mr. Powell will be here in a minute. I let him know you are here already. We have to wait for Mr. Wingate to sign his things too."

Ivy recognized Mr. Wingate as the name of the seller. She straightened her crisp new pink linen suit. Her new pink shoes pinched her toes, and Ivy really wanted nothing more than to kick them off under the table. Instead, she stood and walked to the cooler for a cup of cold water. As she watched the water stream out of the machine, the door opened, and the secretary led in a big man who wore tan Dockers and a cotton plaid short-sleeved shirt. Their eyes met, and recognition brought smiles to both their faces.

"Ivy Chandler from Phoenix?" he asked with a broad smile on his handsome face as he extended his big hand. "You're the person buying my house?"

"Truck driver Dan?" Ivy returned his smile and allowed her hand to be swallowed by his. "I thought you said you were from Victorville, California."

He loosed her hand and joined Ivy at the table. "I am now. My brother lives out there, and after Cindy died, I went out to make it my base of operations for the trucking business."

"I'm sorry for your loss," Ivy told him and took a sip of her water. "I've met a few folks around town, and she was very well-liked."

"Yeah," he smiled sadly, "she was a sweetheart. Everyone loved my Cindy."

"I stopped by the cabin yesterday to look around, and her cousin Peggy stopped by to say hello."

"Watch that one," Dan warned sternly. "If you don't follow her into that church of hers, she'll smear your name all over town."

Ivy laughed. "Dan, I write erotic romances for a living. I doubt I'd be welcome at any church even if I were so inclined. She already invited me, and I respectfully declined."

Dan rolled his eyes. "She's a spiteful bitch. I'd advise you to stear clear of her and her stupid husband, who acts like she has a bit in his mouth and follows her around like a whipped puppy with its tail between its legs. If Peggy says, jump Warren shouts, 'How high, honey?' And don't even get me started on her house full of brats. Cindy watched after them for years free of charge, and Peggy had a long list of rules about how we had to treat 'em."

Dan stood up and got a cup of water. "I was happy when they got old enough to fend for themselves. Thankfully Peggy and Warren put 'em on tractors about the time they turned twelve, and they went to work full time on the farm."

"I doubt she'll be back since I turned down her church invitation."

Mr. Powell came in, apologizing to them for his tardiness. They spent the next forty-five minutes signing papers, making copies, and going over different aspects of the sales contract. Mr. Powell wanted to make certain Ivy understood that if there were any problems with the property, she could not come back on him because she'd opted out of an inspection and was buying the property as-is.

"I left the warranty papers for the roof, the well pump, and all the appliances except that silly cookstove in a drawer in the kitchen," Dan said. "That roof has a lifetime warranty. It's why we bought it."

"Thanks, Dan, I'll look it all over and save it. Is there anything you think I should know about the place?" Ivy asked and dropped her pen back into her purse. Powell's secretary brought her copies of the papers in a manila folder. She stood and offered her hand to Powell. "Thank you, Mr. Powell, for facilitating this transaction on such short notice. It was so very quick and easy."

"My pleasure, Miss Chandler." He took her hand and shook it vigorously. "If there's anything else I can do for you, just let me know. Penny stapled my card to the folder." He opened the door and held it to usher them out. Ivy thought he must have had more business waiting.

Dan stepped aside for her to pass, and Ivy got a nose full of his manly scent. His big, strong body aroused her. She couldn't deny that. He stopped her with an insistent hand on her shoulder, and Ivy noticed he still wore his wedding ring. "Now that all this business is finished, why don't you let me buy you lunch, and then we can run out to the cabin, and I can show you around and give you the particulars about lighting the pilot lights and starting the pump on the well."

Ivy smiled up at him as they walked out into the narrow hall and toward the front of the office. "That would be lovely, but I need to be out at the house by two because the man from the antique store is delivering some things I bought yesterday."

"Humphry?" Dan asked with a frown. "That old rat knows the way. He sold Cindy a ton of his old junk over the years."

"So he told me. He was very fond of her."

"He was very fond of her money." Dan scowled.

"Humphry said you didn't care much for antiques." Ivy laughed merrily as they walked with casual disregard together into the front lobby. Dan put his hand on the small of her back and reached to open the door leading out of Powell's office.

"Ivy?" a familiar voice asked, and Ivy looked over to see Carl Anderson stand. Beside him, sitting straight in one of the narrow tweed-upholstered chairs, was Judith Merriman dressed in an elegant blue Prada suit with a designer bag on her lap. "What are you doing here, Ivy?"

"Hello, Carl." Ivy stared at him, irritated. She hadn't heard from him since the call on her trip across New Mexico.

"If you must know, I just signed the papers for that lovely cabin we looked at." Dan dropped his hand from her back, but Ivy leaned into him for both support and to irritate Carl. Dan returned his hand. "Mr. Powell contacted me when you didn't return his calls about it. I'd just signed the book deal, so I made him an offer on the place. You didn't seem to be interested in it any longer."

"He told me it was sold."

"It is now," Ivy replied curtly. "He told me he'd left you several messages about the other sale falling through, and you never called him back about it. We both finally assumed you were no longer interested, so I made an offer and bought it." Carl stared coldly at Dan, standing beside Ivy with his hand on her back. "This is Dan Wingate, Carl, the previous owner," Ivy said when Carl wouldn't stop glaring at the man. "He's taking me back out to the place to show me how to light the pilot lights and such."

Judith Merriman stood and cleared her throat at Carl's side. She discreetly took his hand, and Ivy knew it was strictly for her benefit.

"Ivy, this is Judith Merriman. She's decided to underwrite this project here in Branson with me."

Ivy extended her hand to the woman. "Of course, your real estate investment friend. I'm Ivy Chandler." Ivy attempted to sound smug and nonchalant. With her head swimming and her heart breaking, she wasn't certain she could pull it off.

Dan gently rubbed the small of her back and pushed Ivy a little toward the open door. "We'd better get going, Ivy, if we're going to get lunch and make it out to the house in time to meet Humphry with your furniture." Dan made the statement to infer familiarity.

"You're absolutely right, Dan." Ivy looked back to a bewildered Carl and gave him one of her sweetest smiles. "We need to get going. My furniture is being delivered this afternoon. Nice to meet you, Mrs. Merriman." Ivy smiled at her sweetly, as well. "Good luck with your condos, Carl."

Ivy let Dan usher her out the door. He walked with her to the Lexus. "We can take my car," Ivy said in a trembling voice. "I need to come back into town to buy some mattresses anyhow." Ivy handed the handsome truck driver the keys. "You can drive. You know your way around town better than I do."

Dan took the keys from her trembling hand and pushed the button that unlocked the door and started the car. Ivy glanced up to see Carl watching them intently from the window. She smiled at Dan as she walked casually around the front of the car and opened the passenger-side door. Ivy dropped into the seat and lifted in her legs that left her unsteady and about to let her fall. She battled back tears as she watched Carl and Judith walk hand in hand behind Norman Powell toward the back of the office.

"Is that old man someone special to you?" Dan asked as he backed her car out of the parking lot.

"He's not that old," Ivy said in defense of Carl. "He's only a few years older than me and probably you."

"Snow on the mountain, but fire down below?" Dan chuckled.

"Something like that. Carl and I were friends. We can leave it at that." Ivy took a tissue from her purse, dabbed at her eyes, and blew her nose.

"Doesn't look that way to me. Who's the blonde? She was surely shootin' daggers with her eyes in your direction."

"He says she's a friend and business associate, but I think it's more than that."

"She sure thinks it is. That's for damned sure." Dan parked the Lexus in front of a block building with a wide, tall window displaying furniture. "You may as well get those mattresses before we get lunch. I don't think you're in the mood for food just now anyhow. You look like you could use some serious retail therapy." They got out of the car, and Dan pushed the button on the key fob that locked it.

Dan took her hand as they walked into the furniture store, and the acrid scent of new furniture and floor wax assaulted Ivy's nose. A salesman in a red jacket walked up and offered his services. He recognized Dan, and they began chatting about his truck and his travels since leaving Branson.

"Mark, this is Ivy Chandler, and she just bought my place. She bought some of that old crap from Humphry and needs new mattresses."

"Nice to meet you, Ms. Chandler." He offered his hand but dropped hers quickly as if he sensed some urgency. "If you'll follow me, the mattresses are right back here. What size do you need?"

"I need a queen and two twin sets. I'd like pillow-tops if you have them. I need a nice sleeper sofa too." They walked to the back of the store, and Ivy was thrilled to find Mayer's also offered a section of the store with a selection of linens for bed, bath, and kitchens.

After she chose three pillow-top mattresses, Dan followed her through the aisles of linens, where Ivy found sheets, pillows, and bedding sets for all the beds. She also picked up towels, washcloths, and accent pieces for the bathroom and kitchen. Ivy had to admit she enjoyed shopping without the restraint of worrying about the prices. Dan had been correct. Retail therapy was precisely what Ivy had needed. She didn't go overboard, however, and only bought the essentials to make the house functional and comfortable.

"Dan, would you happen to know the cabin's window measurements?" Ivy asked as they passed by a display of draperies.

"I don't, but Mark here might be able to look it up. Cindy bought all her curtains here."

Mark looked it up on his computer, and over the next hour, Ivy selected draperies for all the rooms, and a sleeper sofa and matching accent chair. The extra-long brown velour couch had an unusually thick mattress for a sleeper sofa and made out into a queen-size bed. The over-stuffed rolled-arm accent chair was upholstered in a brown and teal fleur-de-lis print along with a matching ottoman. The set was a little modern for her taste, but Ivy thought it would look good in the cabin with the oak tables and shelving she'd purchased from Humphry.

Ivy chose teal drapes to accent the chair, and coffee-stained lace sheers. She chose black iron drapery rods for all the windows in the cabin. Excited to see the things put together in the cabin, Ivy hurried to the counter to pay for her purchases.

"Good God, woman," Dan gasped when Mark gave her the bill, which she paid with her Mastercard, "that erotic romance shit must pay pretty good."

"Sex sells," Ivy said with a giggle as she signed the receipt. Maybe she'd explain things to him later, but for now, Ivy thought she'd let him go on thinking her sexy erotic writing paid for everything and not the historical fiction for which she'd signed the publishing contract.

✻ 14 ✻

They returned to her car, and Dan stopped by his bank to deposit the check from the sale of the cabin. They found a BBQ joint, and Dan bought sandwiches, fries, and a six-pack of Buds to take back to the cabin. They made it before two and ate their lunch sitting next to one another on the porch swing. As they ate and enjoyed a beer, Peggy saw them and pulled her pickup into the drive.

"Oh, shit," Dan groaned upon seeing Peggy's ample backside climbing from the truck. "Here comes the fat bitch from Hell." He chugged his beer and opened another.

Peggy strode up to the porch staring at the two eating together on the swing. "What are you doing here drinking with this woman, Dan Wingate? Cindy's hardly cold in her grave, and you're sitting here sharing alcohol with this ungodly woman. I know my sweet Cindy would be so ashamed." Peggy seethed.

"Peggy, I'm just here to show Miss Chandler how to light the pilots and prime the pump for the well. We had the closing and picked up some food while we wait for Humphry and Mayer's to deliver her furniture." He took a long drink of his beer.

"Cindy wanted me to go on with my life after she passed if it's any of your damned business, Peggy." He stood and pointed at the heavyset, graying woman. "I couldn't say it while Cindy was alive—God only knows why, but she loved you—and I shouldn't really say it now because the cabin's not actually mine anymore," he jabbed the finger repeatedly at the suddenly quaking woman and raised his voice, "but get the hell off this goddamned property, you busy-body, loud-mouth bitch."

Peggy gasped, "Oh, my Lord. You're a drunken, philandering beast, Dan Wingate." She pointed an accusatory finger at Ivy. "And do you know what kind of woman you've sold Cindy's house to? I looked her up online." She glared back at Dan. "She writes trashy filth. Did you know that? Cindy is no doubt rolling in her grave to have such filth moving into her precious home."

"Shut the hell up, Peggy," Dan retorted. "You know damned well Cindy bought and read nothing but that trashy filth because she always passed it all right to you when she was finished with it."

Peggy took a deep breath, turned on her heel, and stomped back to her truck, loudly reciting the twenty-third Psalm as she went.

"I'm the author of trashy filth. I admit that, but," Ivy laughed, "not a demon to be exorcized with Holy Water and the Lord's Prayer."

"You'd better hang chicken feet around the property to keep *that* evil witch away." Dan laughed and finished his beer as Humphry drove up in his panel van.

"Dan Wingate." Humphry smiled and stretched out his hand. "It's so nice to see you. I hope you're here to help us unload Miss Ivy's purchases, though I know you're not very fond of antiques. But I have to tell you that Miss Cindy would have loved everything going back into her little house."

It irritated Ivy some that everyone still referred to this as Cindy's house. Maybe after she got it furnished and decorated, people would come to see it as Ivy Chandler's house.

Over the next hour, Dan, Humphry, Humphry's grandson, and Ivy carried in the antiques. Things were stacked into their appropriate rooms for Ivy to arrange later at her leisure. Dan made certain the beds were assembled so the mattresses could be installed upon their arrival. The truck from Mayer's arrived as Humphry's backed out of the drive.

The big pieces came in first, then the bags with the linens and accessories. Ivy looked around at the sofa and chair, the antique lamps resting upon the end tables, the boxes of china on the oak dining table, and the stuffed deer head leaning against the fireplace. She couldn't wait to get started putting things together. From her car, Ivy retrieved the suitcases she'd loaded into it that morning from her hotel room and carried them into the cabin.

"Are you ready to go back to town?" Ivy asked Dan after the Mayer's men left in their delivery truck.

"Don't you need help setting all this shit up? Just tell me where you want it, and I'll move it for ya." He glanced around the big living room, now filled with what he considered junk. He took the bundle of curtain rods and began cutting away the plastic tape holding them together. "If you have a screwdriver, I'll hang these for ya."

Ivy tossed him the car key again. "There's a tool kit in the trunk."

"Consider it done." He walked out onto the porch, and Ivy carried the bags of linens into her bedroom. She began separating the bedding and moving it to the respective rooms. Ivy made up the two twin beds in the guest room then returned to her bedroom.

She tore off the plastic from the expensive pink Egyptian-cotton sheets with their delicate scalloped embroidery along the top edge. When she had them on the thick pillow-top mattress, the top sheet hung down just over the edge of the white eyelet bed ruffle. Ivy took the folded chenille spread and draped it over the back of the rocker sitting in the corner. She stepped back to admire the shabby chic furnishings, their off-white bright against the bare logs of the outer wall.

Cindy had painted the inside sheetrock walls a pale shade of sage green, and it highlighted the faux-finished furniture. A color Ivy would have chosen herself; she began to appreciate Cindy Wingate's taste. Perhaps she too would continue to think of this as Cindy's house for a little while longer.

With the beds made and Dan back inside, screwing rod brackets onto the walls, Ivy carried towels into the bathroom. A door opened from Ivy's bedroom as well as from the living room into the only bathroom in the cabin. She piled the black iron-looking accessories upon the counter between the double sinks.

"Dan, would you mind taking down these old towel bars and replacing them with these new ones?"

Dan poked his head into the bathroom. "Sure, no problem." He smiled at her with the screwdriver in his hand. "Almost feels like bein' married again."

She glanced at him, stunned for a moment. "I'm so sorry, Dan. If this makes you feel weird, I'll take you back to town now." Ivy's face flushed with shame, embarrassed by her thoughtlessness. "I should have considered how this must be hurting you being back in her house, putting curtain rods and things up for another woman."

"Not at all." Dan took her hand. "This is probably the best therapy I could have asked for. Cindy's gone, and putting things up in here for you sort of gives me closure or something." He turned and went back to her drapery rods.

From the bathroom, Ivy moved on to the kitchen, where she began removing the newspaper protecting the delicate English porcelain. Most of the upper cabinets had clear glass panes in the doors, and she arranged the colorful dishes into an appealing display. Arranging the tea service with its sugar bowl, creamer, cups, and dainty saucers gave her particular pleasure. She felt like a little girl playing at having a fancy tea party, and it made her smile. Ivy hung dish towels over the oven pull. She added a metal tea kettle upon the repurposed antique stove, not for use but as a decorative piece.

In the center of the round oak table, Ivy spread a crocheted doily and positioned a large ceramic bowl and pitcher. These were nowhere near the beautiful set Carl had in his bedroom and were definitely from the 1960s when colonial reproductions had been popular decorative accents.

Ivy remembered her mother having one much like it in their home as a child. Humphry could sell it as an antique because it was more than fifty years old, though not of the actual period represented. It was pretty, however, and went with the look Ivy wanted to achieve in her new country home.

Her eyes took in the lovely kitchen and made her smile. The green gingham curtains weren't hung yet, but Ivy was pleased with the accomplishments thus far. She heard Dan curse from the other room and peeked around the corner to see him standing in the doorway of the guest bedroom, alternately shaking his left hand then sucking on the thumb of the same.

"Are you OK?" Ivy called to him.

"Yeah, I was putting up the rod in here and got a damned splinter." He sucked at his thumb again. "I kept telling Cindy we should drywall these outside walls, but she insisted on keeping the logs visible. It's not practical. They should have been studded and insulated, but she claimed it would ruin the appeal of having a log cabin if you couldn't see the actual logs." He sighed and returned to his project.

Ivy had to agree with her predecessor but flushed with guilt for forcing this sweet man to recall the wonderful life he'd had here with his late wife. Was she being cruel or, as he'd said, allowing him to find closure? Ivy began scooting the living room furniture around on the plank floor, careful of scratching the finely polished wood. When she had the tables where she wanted them, Ivy rearranged hurricane lamps, plugging the ones that had been converted to electricity into the wall sockets.

The power company had turned on the electricity sometime that morning. Having gone to the local utility office the day before and paid the deposit, she'd asked for the electricity to be turned back on as soon as possible. It had relieved her to find the meter still on the house, so there would be no need for an inspection by the county. When they'd arrived after the closing, Dan and Ivy had noticed the light on the porch glowing and the paddles of the ceiling fan turning slowly.

Dan had gone to the well house, turned on the pump, and shown her how to pour water into the top to prime it. She'd gone into the cabin then to turn off all the faucets once the water began to run through the drained pipes.

Dan turned the valve on the big propane tank sitting behind the house to allow the gas to flow and went inside and showed Ivy how to light the pilots on the gas furnace, water heater, and kitchen stove. She was happy to find the fireplace burned only wood, and Dan showed her how to work the damper so the cabin wouldn't fill with smoke.

Ivy watched him walk into her bedroom with his screwdriver. She was eager to hang the long lace panels over the window, looking out onto the green hedge, hanging full of white five-petal roses. She'd opened the window, hoping their scent would fill the room.

"Will you hang that rod close to the ceiling? I bought extra-long drapes to give the illusion of a tall French window in here."

Dan gave her a frown of mock frustration. "Yes, ma'am. Just let me get a chair from the kitchen to stand on and hope I don't break Humphry's piece of old junk with my weight." He tossed the screwdriver onto the bed and stepped by Ivy, brushing her bare shoulder. His man-scent excited her, and her eyes followed his shapely behind as he left the room.

Get hold of yourself, Chandler. He must feel weird enough being in his wife's house with another woman as it is. He doesn't need to contend with some horny old cougar as well.

Dan walked back in, the muscles in his upper arms bulging as he carried the oak Windsor chair back from the kitchen. Ivy thought about Carl and how he must have labored at decorating his condo in Arizona. He must have climbed plenty of ladders or step stools to put together things the way he had.

I wonder what he had in mind for this place. I'm sure he must have had some ideas. I suppose I'll never know now.

Ivy watched Dan's gorgeous body as he stepped up onto the chair, careful not to overturn it as he climbed.

"You're gonna have to hand me the screwdriver and the brackets. I have the screws in my pocket." Ivy watched him take a measuring tape and pencil from his pocket. He used the tape to measure from the edge of the ceiling. "Does this look about right?" He held the pencil about eight inches down from the ceiling and four inches over from the edge of the window casing.

Ivy stepped back to gauge the height. If the lace puddled on the floor, it would actually look more proper to the period. "That looks great. Cindy taught you well."

He turned and smiled down at her. "I got to admit that she did. I know all about measuring for drapes, hanging pictures at eye level, and hanging the pictures in groups with similar frames. She taught me lots of tricks."

"If she read books like the ones I write," Ivy raised an eyebrow and giggled slyly, "I bet she did."

"Oh, man." He stepped down to move the chair to the other side of the window. "That woman came up with some freaky shit after reading some of those books," he said and laughed. "Do y'all write from experience or just your imaginations?" Ivy watched him measure and mark again before screwing the black metal bracket onto the uneven log wall.

"A little bit of both." Ivy pushed the rod into the pocket at the top of the lace draperies. The roses in the weave had been tinted shades of pink and the foliage soft green, almost the same shade as the painted walls. Ivy had chosen them because they reminded her of the painted mirror now hanging over the antique bureau.

The shabby chic room dripped pastels. The little girl in Ivy, who'd always wanted one of those frilly canopy beds, jumped with joy, while the antique purist in her cringed a bit, looking at the mishmash of painted styles jammed together in one setting.

From the pink roses delicately stenciled on the panel doors of the tall wardrobe to the floral topiaries on the bureau, and the roses in the lace draperies, the room was a little girl's dream room. Ivy had never been one for unicorns and rainbows, but she had always been a fool for pastel florals, lace, and satin ribbons.

Ivy handed Dan the rod with the curtains hanging from it, and he placed it into the brackets. Black fleur-de-lis finials kept the drapes from slipping over the ends. Ivy cast her eyes around the beautiful room with pride. It had turned out better than she could have hoped.

Dan took his screwdriver into the bathroom and began replacing the old towel bars, toilet paper holder, and shower rod with the new black ones. Ivy thought she might replace the faucet sets with the black antique-looking ones she'd seen at the Home Depot once. The farmer's sink in the kitchen would look great with one of those big black gooseneck faucets and the four-pronged porcelain handles she so admired. The cabinet doors in the kitchen should have porcelain pulls to match those on the pie safe to bring it all together.

Ivy hung the fluffy white towels upon the new towel bars and hand towels on the rings beside each sink. She slid the shower rod through the pocket of a curtain that matched her bedroom curtains. She hadn't been certain about making the bath too girly, but what the hell. It was her house. If she liked and wanted girly, so be it.

"Do you have any other pictures or what-nots you want hung in here?" Dan asked as he shoved the screwdriver into his back pocket.

"Not at the moment." His handsome face, beginning to sprout some late afternoon stubble, made her smile. "Once I get all the major stuff situated, I'll go back to Humphry's for the finishing touches."

"You're fixin' to become that old man's favorite person." He chuckled. "He's a real charmer to women with fat purses." Dan returned to the living room, where Ivy saw him lift the deer head to mount on the river-rock fireplace above the heavy oak mantel. It went up quickly as a hook had already been mounted there that he knew about. "You should get some mounted bass and maybe some stuffed ducks or a turkey for in here." He nodded to indicate the living room.

"I was thinking about doing up the guest room with that sort of thing," she called back to him as she hung toilet paper. "I got those blue and green plaid drapes and bedspreads for in there. A couple of mounted fish on the wall would be great to give it that hunting retreat look. I'll put it on my list. I think I saw a couple at Humphry's place."

"Figures," he grumbled and furrowed his brow.

15

The sun had set when they got into the Lexus to drive back into town, both exhausted.

"Do you want to stop for dinner?" Dan asked her as they backed out of the drive onto the narrow asphalt road.

"Can there possibly be anyplace better than that BBQ we had for lunch?"

"There's a pretty good steak joint downtown," Dan offered.

Ivy looked down at her dusty jeans and dustier t-shirt that had not been dusty at all when she'd changed into them before their lunch on the swing. "I'm not really dressed for a fancy steak place. How about Chinese?"

"There's a Panda Express over by the movie theatre. Is that OK? They don't serve beer."

"That's alright," Ivy replied. "I'll be driving back in the dark and don't need to be drinking."

"That's smart." He turned down a street and into a strip mall with a brightly lit movie theatre as the anchor unit. Restaurants, coffee shops, an ice cream parlor, and a used book store flanked the tall structure on either side. Cars filled the parking lot. Dan parked close to the Panda Express, and they walked in together. Most of the tables were full, and many people recognized and waved at Dan.

The woman behind the counter greeted them and filled their plates with fried rice, broccoli beef, and orange chicken. Ivy asked for crab puffs and an eggroll as well. Dan got them Sprites while she paid for the food. Ivy didn't mind. She figured she owed him for all his back-breaking labor. He hadn't needed to stay after getting the pump going and lighting the pilots, but he had, and Ivy didn't know what she would have done without his assistance. She certainly wouldn't have drapes on all the windows, that was certain.

"Thanks for all your help today, Dan," Ivy said as he sat and handed her the Sprite, a napkin, and a plastic fork. "I really don't know what I would have done without your help today."

"It's no trouble." He forked up some beef that dripped savory brown sauce back onto his heaping plate. "I figured I owed you anyhow."

"What do you mean?"

"Well, I was really rude to you back at that truck stop." He handed her a crab puff from his plate. "And I ate your chips."

"Do you actually pick up many women at truck stops that way?" Ivy asked with a sheepish grin as she popped a bite of tangy orange chicken into her mouth with some rice.

"Not usually. Most places are crawling with lot-lizards that only the most desperate pay to stick their cocks into. I don't mess with that trash, but you looked beautiful and lonely sittin' there in that booth." He sucked up some soda. "I thought I'd give it a go, but you shot me down."

"Did you ever get lucky?"

"Not until this morning when I saw you sittin' there in Norm's office all dressed up and lookin' like a million bucks."

"Thanks, but you didn't really get lucky. You just got dragged into moving furniture and hanging curtain rods in your old house full of sad memories."

"That's not true." He took the hand Ivy wasn't using. "Being back in that house and watching you having so much fun decorating the way Cindy did was great for me. I felt alive again for the first time since watching her take her last breath in that damned hospital bed." Dan reluctantly dropped her hand and returned to his food. "And getting the chance to tell Peggy Martin to get the hell out of my shit was a blessing I really hadn't planned on," he said and laughed.

"You know she's gonna be back down there beggin' you for books the first chance she gets. She knew exactly when Cindy was finished with one and was right there on the porch with her hand out. I don't think that woman's ever paid for a book unless it was fifty cents at a yard sale."

"She'll get no freebies from me. Authors make their money from the royalties when their books *sell.*"

"Don't they pay you big money to write them?" he asked, dumbfounded.

"Some authors get paid an *advance* against royalties if the publisher thinks the work is marketable. The author doesn't collect any royalties until that advance has been collected back by the publisher from the sales." Ivy bit into the crispy crust of the eggroll after dipping it into the tangy sweet and sour sauce. "Miss Peggy will get no free books from me."

"Good." Dan sucked the last of his soda from his cup.

They finished up, and Dan held her chair as she stood.

A gentleman, after all? I'm spent, or I think I'd offer to have him take me back home and spend the night.

Ivy drove him back to his truck at Norman Powell's office. He walked around to the driver's door, and Ivy lowered the window.

"I had a very nice day, Ivy Chandler. May I see you again?" He leaned in and kissed her.

It wasn't a passionate kiss at first, but it wasn't a peck on the cheek either. Ivy didn't pull away and allowed the kiss to go on longer than either of them had expected. He reached in and put his hand on the back of her head, pulling her closer for a moment as their tongues twined around one another's and their lips pressed tighter.

"Wow, now that was a goodnight kiss," he whispered before standing and walking to his truck.

Ivy sat in the Lexus, breathless from the unexpected kiss, and watched the pickup back out of the parking lot and drive away. She backed out as well and made her way to the cabin without encountering any stray deer along the way, to her great relief.

Twice since arriving in the rural area, the sleek animals had darted in front of her car from the tall grasses or woods along the way to the cabin. Ivy didn't want to hit one and injure it or wreck her new car. She found herself driving slowly and keeping her eyes on the edges of the narrow roads, looking for the reflection of her headlights in waiting eyes.

As she pulled into her drive, Ivy was surprised to see the reflection of tail lights from another vehicle. In the glow of the porch light, Ivy saw the white head of Carl Anderson sitting in one of the wicker chairs. Ivy rolled her eyes, shifted the car into park, and stepped out.

"Hello, Carl. What are you doing here?" Ivy stepped up onto the porch, opened the screen door, and unlocked the heavy door leading into the cabin. She glanced over to Carl, who still sat, swatting at buzzing mosquitos attracted by the light. "Are you coming in, or do you plan to stay out here with the mosquitos?"

Carl stood and followed Ivy into the cabin. They walked into a fully furnished room decorated with a few antique lamps, a stuffed deer head, and a mantel clock ticking loudly. The ceiling fan set on low turned lazily above their heads, circulating the heavy, moist Missouri air. Glowing bulbs in the mock-antique fixture attached to the fan shined down on Dan and Ivy's accomplishments.

On the wall above the sofa hung a four-foot painting of a forest scene at dusk or dawn, the sky tinted in shades of pink and orange. It was one of the few frivolous decorative items Ivy had purchased from Humphry's store, and she loved the way it accented the wall painted in the same shade of green as her bedroom, the bath, and the kitchen.

Ivy thought back to Dan and wondered if her and Cindy's tastes had more similarities than only decorating. Carl cleared his throat and brought Ivy back to the moment at hand.

"The place looks nice," Carl said, looking up at the wide rack of antlers on the deer above his head. "It didn't take you long to pull things together. Where'd you find all this stuff?"

"I had a day or so before the closing, so I found an antique mall and bought some furniture. I'm leaving the stuff in Phoenix there. My sister's going to have it put into storage for me. I'm driving back in a week or two to pick up Cheshire and a few other things."

"So, you've decided to stay here?" Carl asked as he walked into the kitchen and flipped on the light switch. "This looks good. Lots of green, but it looks good." Ivy had chosen dark green gingham curtains for the kitchen that were the same shade of Irish green as the kitchen cabinets. Cindy's light green coated the walls except for the end wall with its chinked redwood logs.

"It's my favorite color," Ivy said flatly. "It seems the woman who lived here before liked a lot of the same things I do."

"Her husband tell you that?" he sneered. Carl left the kitchen and went through the rest of the cabin, turning on lights to see what Ivy had done with the rooms.

Ivy followed him. "Him, the man at the antique store, the guy at the furniture store, and her cousin from up the road," she snapped.

"Already met that many people, have you?" Carl walked into her bedroom and flipped the wall switch. The light blazed on to highlight the white-painted furniture and pastel palate of the very feminine room. Ivy followed his eyes around as he took in every painted piece of furniture. As an antique purist, Ivy knew Carl's stomach probably turned at what he would consider an abomination and defiling of fine furniture. "Are you kidding me? What the hell is this mess supposed to be?" Carl sneered.

"It's my bedroom."

"It looks like Cinderella and Jane Austen got together for a play date."

"Oh, please." Ivy rolled her eyes.

Carl shook his head, walked past her and down the hall to the guest bedroom. Ivy turned off her bedroom light and dropped into the plush chair in the living room. He peeked into the bathroom before taking a seat on the couch. "The bathroom's about as bad as the bedroom. I never took you for the frustrated romantic type."

"You've never really spent enough time with me to take me for anything, Carl. Where's Judith? I'm sure she will probably do a wonderful job decorating the condos for you."

"Judith went back to Phoenix after the closing. We flew here in her company plane, and she had to get back to the boys." He gave Ivy a sullen glare. "Judith is a business associate and a good friend."

"Right," Ivy snapped, "a friend with great boobs, a great ass, a million-dollar company, *and* a private plane." She stomped into the bathroom so Carl couldn't see the tears seeping from her eyes. Ivy pulled herself together, blew her nose, and returned to the living room. "What do you want, Carl?"

"I wanted to apologize for not telling you I was back in town and not returning your calls." He scratched his head. "It was rude and inconsiderate. And I should have told you about Judith."

Ivy cut him off. "Judith was none of my business. She's much more suited to your social circles than I am. I understand that." Ivy wiped her nose again and batted back the new tears stinging her eyes. "I *was* hurt that you let me think you were in Wisconsin with your grandkids when you were actually in town with her. I had to find out about it in the paper, for God's sake."

"I thought you might have seen that, but like I said before, we never had anything more than a friends-with-benefits sort of thing." He stood and motioned around the room. "I never should have taken you on that trip and brought you here. I didn't mean to lead you on or make you think there was more of a future for us than what there was in Phoenix."

"That's just great, Carl." Ivy's temper began to boil over. "Just great. If your plane left town without you, how were you planning to get home?"

"I thought maybe I could catch a ride with you," Carl said calmly.

Ivy stared at him, open-mouthed. "You're shitting me, right? You didn't even know I was here. How were you planning on getting home before you saw me here?"

"Well, Judith was going to stay a bit longer, but she decided she needed to get back to the boys."

"Oh, I see." Ivy didn't see. "Carl, I'm going to be staying here. I may go back to the valley when it gets cold, but I don't know yet."

"But that's great, baby. You'll be here to do the management of the rentals like we talked about before." He looked around the big living room. "We can get you a little office space set up over there in the corner, and you can take care of the reservations and the advertising."

"Carl, stop," Ivy interrupted. "I'm going to be concentrating on my writing. My agent says they'll be sending me around to bookstores doing signings once they launch the first book. She's talked them into a major promotional campaign, and I don't think I'm going to have time to be your secretary."

"But I thought you wanted to have a relationship with me." He looked awestruck at her refusal.

"I did, but not just a business relationship. I want a man who wants to have me on his arm at award dinners and not just in his bed as an after-thought or taking care of his properties. I deserve better than that. I deserve to be loved."

"And you think you're going to find love out here

in Hillbilly Heaven?" He laughed. "You couldn't find it begging for dates on the internet back in Phoenix. What makes you think you'll find it out here in the sticks?"

They were interrupted by a knock on the door. Ivy stormed past Carl and opened the door to see a cleanly shaven Dan Wingate standing on her porch. "Am I interrupting something here?" he asked as he walked in past Ivy and saw Carl on the couch.

"Yes," Carl snapped rudely.

"No, Carl was just leaving," Ivy snapped back, holding the door, and glaring at the red-faced Carl. "We've said all we have to say to one another."

Carl stood and strode past Ivy out the door without speaking. She heard the door on his rental car slam and gravel spray as he backed out of the drive.

"What's his problem?" Dan asked. He took Ivy's hand, pried her fingers from the brass knob, and shut the door. "Are you alright, Ivy? What's going on?" He took a clean white cotton handkerchief from the pocket of his clean jeans and handed it to her when he saw tears sliding down her pale cheeks.

Ivy took the handkerchief with trembling fingers and wiped away the tears with haste. "Thanks." She took a deep breath and wiped at her nose. "Carl and I just had a final parting of ways."

"I didn't think you two were going together."

"We weren't really." Ivy went on to explain to Dan about her on-again-off-again relationship with Carl and how he'd assumed she would jump at the chance to work for him here in Branson. Ivy got them both glasses of ice water. "I'm sorry I don't have anything stronger. I haven't been to the grocery store yet."

"We can take care of that if you want to run into Wal-Mart. It's open all night."

"I'd rather shop at the local market."

"Frank Parson will appreciate that. He runs the IGA and loses a lot of business to Wal-Mart since it started selling groceries."

"I'm sure he does." Ivy handed him the glass of water, ice cubes tinkling against the sides of the tumbler. "I'll run into town in the morning to stock up. So what brought you all the way back out here tonight?" She sat down next to him on the comfortable couch.

"Honestly?" he asked with a sheepish grin.

"Always. I'm too damned old for games and bullshit anymore. Just be honest with me. Please." Ivy took a long drink of the icy water.

"It was that kiss." He took her by the chin, leaned in, and kissed her again. This time Ivy felt the passion, without any doubt. She didn't know if it was needed or if it was just her anger at Carl, but she returned the fiery kiss. Their lips did not part for some time, and their hands began exploring one another's bodies beneath their clothes. Ivy could smell fresh shampoo and knew Dan had showered and changed before returning to see her.

"Wait a minute," he said, pulling away. "I don't want to take advantage. I don't want to be the guy you screw because you're pissed at that other guy you screw." He moved away from her and picked up his water. "I may have come out here lookin' to get laid, but I don't want it like that. Does that make sense, or does it make me sound like an idiot?"

"It makes you sound like you have more integrity than other men I screw," Ivy said with a grin.

"If you're talking about that Carl guy, then I agree. He sounds like nothing but a user to me."

"I guess I never saw it before, but I think he is." Ivy yawned and stretched. "My mom used to say that rich men didn't get rich passing around their money. They stay rich by getting as much as they can for nothing. I guess Carl thought because he was getting one thing from me for nothing, he could get more."

"That's just not right. You're a beautiful, smart woman any man would be proud to have. Is he a rich guy?"

"I don't know. He lives like one and does big business deals all over the country. He just bought two condos by the lake here and paid almost a million dollars for them."

"But didn't he say that blonde was underwriting the deal? Doesn't underwriting mean the same as financing?"

"I think it does. Well, I guess she's his business partner now or something. He says she flew back to Phoenix and left him here to get the condos furnished and decorated. He wanted me to give him a ride back home."

"Ballsy," Dan said with a laugh.

"Yeah, that's what I thought." Ivy emptied her glass of water. "So, what is it you're looking for, Dan, besides getting laid?"

He stared at her with a deep furrow above the bridge of his nose. "It's been over a year since Cindy passed, and she was sick for two years with chemo and radiation treatments for the cancer. Don't get me wrong, she was a trooper through all of it, and I'd give anything to have her here, but I miss having a woman in my life." He took a breath. "Not just for the sex. I can get sex anytime I want it, but having a woman to come home to every night and curl up next to is different. You know what I'm talking about?"

"Yes, I do." Ivy reached for his hand. "I'd hoped to have that with Carl, but I think he thought I was just looking for a sugar daddy."

"You don't need one of those, do you?"

"Not anymore, but I sort of did when I first met him. I only just recently signed with a publisher and came into some cash."

"You're still the same person, though. I didn't know you had money when I saw you at the truck stop and liked you right off. You're beautiful, and you're smart. I like that in a woman."

"And *you* have integrity." Ivy leaned over and kissed him gently on his full, soft mouth. "I like that in a man."

Dan leaned into her, wrapped his muscular arms around her, and pulled Ivy close. "You smell good, woman," he whispered, nuzzling her ear beneath her dusty and sweat-stiff hair.

"Now I know that's not true." Ivy stared into his hazel eyes, chuckling. "Unless you like the smell of sweaty, dust-caked women." Ivy stood and took his big hand. "I need a shower. I can tell you've just had one." She ran her fingers through his damp curls then down to caress his smooth, freshly shaven face. "You don't need to join me, but you can watch," Ivy teased and pulled him toward the bathroom.

"You're a tease, woman," he said and smiled as he rose to follow Ivy into the girly pastel bathroom. "I like that in a woman too."

16

Ivy woke early with the sunlight filtering through the lacy drapes into her eyes. It took her a moment to get her bearings and remember where she was. She attempted to roll on her side and rise, but an arm lay across her belly, pinning her to the mattress. Soft, even snores breathed from beside her head, and Ivy turned to see the serene, handsome face and tousled brown hair of Dan Wingate asleep beside her.

"Mornin'," he mumbled when he felt her move beneath his arm. He used the muscular limb over her mid-section to pull Ivy closer into his warm, naked body.

Something stirred in Ivy, and she rolled to face him. Their lips met in a soft kiss of new familiarity. Dan's rough hand found a breast and began pinching a nipple until she shivered and moaned with delight. During the night, they'd explored one another, finding the erogenous zones that elicited the pleasurable moans and erotic responses from one another. Ivy found his heavy balls and used her fingernails to tease with light scratches until she felt his penis firming against her leg, oozing pre-cum.

Dan rolled her onto her back. "You're a devil, woman. You drive me mad with lust." He straddled Ivy's slim hips and used a knee to push her legs apart. She opened herself to him gladly and moaned with pleasure as he entered her.

"Oh, my god. That feels so good." Though tender from their multiple couplings the night before, Ivy arched her back up to meet his ardent thrusts and clenched her vaginal walls to tighten around his thick cock.

"Keep doin' that. I love it," he said, panting above her.

Ivy complied but found herself lost in the pleasure he wrought, sliding between her thighs. Soon her groin exploded with multiple bursts of exquisite delight, and she groaned and moaned with each shuddering blast, causing her body to shiver and stiffen at the same time. "Oh, my God, Dan. Don't stop." Ivy dug her fingers into the pillows behind her head and breathed heavily. "Don't you dare fucking stop."

"Here it comes, woman," he yelled and pounded hard as he exploded into her. He rolled off her sweaty body, panting and spent. "Damn, you suck the cum right out of me the way you clench that thing up on my cock." He ran his hand through her sweat-damp brunette waves.

Ivy lay next to him with an arm raised over her head on the pillow, smiling. "You fuck nice." He didn't respond, and Ivy heard him begin to snore softly beside her. She snatched tissues from the box beside the bed and wiped him from between her legs. Ivy rose and went into the bathroom to relieve herself. The warm afterglow of pleasurable sex radiated through her body. She took a quick shower to wash away the sweat and residue from the night before then dressed quickly and quietly in jeans and a tank top.

She peeked at the bed to see Dan wrapped in the sheet and curled on his side, sleeping soundly. After their night of bedroom Olympics, Ivy thought he'd probably sleep for a good while longer. Her phone read eight forty-five. She grabbed her purse, locked the door to the cabin, and drove into town to find the IGA.

The grocery store's parking lot only had a few cars parked near the entrance, and the store's aisles were all but empty. Ivy noted the aromas of freshly baked bread coming from the bakery, ground coffee from the deli, the sickly sweet scent of over-ripe produce, and harsh detergents. They were the familiar scents assaulting the nose in every small grocery store Ivy could remember entering.

Her cart filled in no time at all. With her house empty of everything for her basic everyday needs, Ivy found herself taking things from every aisle she traveled down. When finished, she had enough bags to fill the empty trunk of the Lexus.

As she drove home, Ivy passed an Ace Hardware with a dazzling display of patio furniture out in front. She stopped and found new cushions for the wicker set and her porch swing. The cushions, bright red and printed with yellow tropical flowers and green foliage, grabbed Ivy's attention immediately. While not exactly fitting her country motif, they did fit the Victorian period with those folks' love of all things tropical.

More elegant Victorian homes would have had a solarium with tropical plants, birds, and wicker displayed throughout. Ivy stuffed the cushions and a few other purchases into the back seat of the car and drove home.

As she turned the Lexus into the gravel drive, Ivy saw Dan sitting in the porch swing. He had one big hand wrapped around the chain, holding the swing with his head resting upon his arm. The swing moved slowly back and forth, but Ivy thought he must be dozing. His head popped up, and he rose when Ivy shut the door and walked around to begin dragging plastic grocery bags from the trunk of the car.

"Did you get coffee?" he asked as he joined her, two big hands picking up the loaded bags.

"Yes, and I got a Mr. Coffee, too. It's in the back seat with the new cushions for the patio furniture." Ivy smiled and carried her load into the kitchen. She filled the refrigerator with sundries like grapefruit juice, milk, mayo, mustard, pickles, and butter.

Quick meals like pot pies went into the freezer along with some cuts of meat, a large bag of frozen fruit for smoothies, and a quart of butter pecan ice cream for those late nights when she needed something cold and sweet that wasn't necessarily healthy.

Ivy would collect her rugged Ninja blender when she returned to retrieve Cheshire, but she bought a Mr. Coffee because she needed her coffee every day. She couldn't go without that until the trip back to Arizona. Dan carried in the box with the coffee maker and ripped it open while Ivy continued to put groceries into the tall pantry next to the refrigerator.

At Humphry's, Ivy had purchased several different sizes of clear and blue-green tinted glass jars with clamping crock lids to use as canisters for flour, sugar, and coffee. She would fill those later. Ivy knew she could perfectly repurpose the old jars in her country kitchen.

She handed Dan the plastic tub of Folger's and watched him set up the coffee maker on the counter by the sink and fill it with water, a paper filter, and the pungent ground beans. Soon the pot filled, and the aroma of brewing coffee inundated the rustic cabin.

"Shall we take our coffee on the veranda, ma'am?" he asked gallantly in an exaggerated Southern accent.

"Why, that would be most lovely, good sir," she replied, smiling. "Do y'all need sugar or cream?"

"No, ma'am, I take mine straight."

Ivy took delicate porcelain cups and saucers from the cabinet and placed them upon a wicker tray. When the Mr. Coffee sputtered its last, Dan added the pot to the tray and switched off the machine. He picked up the tray and carried it out onto the porch and sat it upon the glass top of the wicker table between the two peacock-backed chairs.

Ivy was surprised to see the bright new cushions on the wicker settee and swing as well. The vibrant cushions looked perfect against the natural color of the wicker furniture. Ivy was glad it hadn't been painted white like so many pieces she'd seen.

They settled into the cushioned seats to enjoy their coffee. As they took their first sips, Peggy and her husband drove by in their pickup, glaring. Dan, sitting bare-chested, smiled and waved boldly at the passing truck.

"Dan Wingate, you're a troublemaker," Ivy said, laughing as she watched Peggy throw gravel with her tires as she fishtailed away down the side of the road.

"She's a busy-body old bitch," Dan said as he poured another cup of coffee for himself and topped Ivy's off. "By Monday morning, after she flaps her mouth down at that church of hers, the whole town will know we've been keepin' company. Lord only knows how she'll blow it out of proportion."

"How much more could she blow it? You spent the whole day here yesterday and then the night. You're half-dressed and sitting on my porch drinking coffee. What's she supposed to think?" Ivy said with a giggle as she sipped her coffee and enjoyed the quiet morning.

"She's supposed to mind her own damned business and keep her big mouth shut." Dan drained his cup. "You have anything special you want to do today?"

"I planned to get groceries today, and that's done. I don't have anything else in particular planned. How about you? When do you have to be back on the road?"

Dan stretched his muscular body, scratched his head, and yawned. "I'm having the truck serviced. They won't be finished with it for a couple of days, and then I need to head back to Victorville and see what's up. You planning to head back to Arizona anytime soon?"

"I need to go pick up my cat and some personal items I don't want put into storage, then I'm coming back here for a while to finish the final book in the series."

"You're planning to stay here full time then?" he asked as he emptied the pot into their cups.

"I think so." Ivy stared out at the green field and the trees waving in the gentle late-morning breeze. The scent of the hedge roses wafted across the porch, and she took a deep breath. "I love it here. I'm a Midwestern girl and miss the green. I miss the changing of the seasons. Winters should be cold. I mean really cold, not just fifty degrees at night."

"Yeah," Dan said and laughed, "isn't it freaky how desert people get all bundled up in heavy coats when it drops below seventy? I laughed my ass off at my brother and his wife when they turned the furnace on because it was supposed to drop down into the sixties one night. I was walkin' around in shorts and flip-flops while they wore sweaters and heavy socks. I couldn't believe it."

Ivy huffed. "And I think it gets colder up in Victorville than it does in Phoenix, but people there are the same," she said. "I've never owned anything heavier than a tweed jacket the whole time I've lived out there and only wear shoes when I'm going out."

"You want to go with me in the truck to pick up your stuff?" Dan asked.

Ivy shook her head. "I have to get my cat. He doesn't like to travel and would probably really freak out in your big, loud truck. I'm not bringing back too much, so it should fit into the back of my car easily enough. I just have some kitchen stuff, some pictures, a few clothes, and Cheshire. My sister is really upset with me, so I need to spend a little time with her before I come back."

"She's not happy about the move?" Dan reached over and gave her arm a gentle caress.

Ivy rolled her blue eyes and smiled. "That would be putting it mildly." Ivy took his hand and held it in hers. Having Dan nearby to touch was comforting and gave her a sense of well-being she'd never felt with Carl. He'd always made her feel self-conscious and unsure of herself. With Dan, she felt at ease. She didn't know him at all, really, but it felt as though they'd known one another for years when they were together.

"My brother probably won't like it when I tell him I've decided to come back here either."

"Are you thinking about it?" Ivy asked with surprise.

He tightened the grip on her hand. "I am now."

"Oh my." Ivy gulped. "I had no idea. Are you regretting selling me the house now?"

"Not at all," he exclaimed. "*You're* the reason I'm thinking about coming back. I've got nothing holding me in California, and I can run the truck from here … well not," he pointed at the cabin, "here, here, but here in Branson somewhere." He grinned. "I heard there were going to be some nice condos on the lake for rent soon."

"Yeah, right," Ivy said and chuckled. She glanced back through the window into the homey cabin. "Why *not* here?" she asked him, nervous he might think her bold for suggesting. "You know the place. That would be a big help to me, and it would certainly give Peggy something to talk about."

Dan stared back at her open-mouthed. "Seriously? You'd consider having me live here with you? You don't even know me that well yet. I might be a psychotic serial killer or something."

Ivy giggled, remembering how she'd thought precisely that about him when they'd met at the truck stop. "We know one another well enough to sleep together. I don't know about you, but I certainly enjoyed it." Ivy began putting the coffee cups back onto the tray. "Anyhow, it's not like you'd be here with me all the time. You'll be gone with your truck for weeks at a time." She stood and picked up the tray. "This would be more like a pit-stop along the way between runs."

"It certainly would be something to stick in that old bitch Peggy's craw." Dan leaned his head back and belly-laughed.

"Yes, it would." Ivy chuckled and carried the tray back into her house.

17

Ivy made her trip back to Arizona to collect Cheshire two weeks before the Labor Day weekend. Vacation traffic on the highways had eased, and gas prices had fallen. She hoped to be on her way back before they went up again for the busy travel weekend.

Her sister scolded her harshly for being impetuous and making expensive decisions without giving them careful thought. Ivy knew what Carrie really meant was Ivy's making expensive decisions without consulting *her* first. She grumbled about having to deal with Cheshire and packing up Ivy's things and cleaning up her apartment. She loved her sister, but the constant nagging and complaining finally hit Ivy's last nerve, and she loaded up her suitcases, boxes, and cat into the Lexus to get back out onto the road to Branson. Ivy kissed her weeping sister goodbye and took off only four days after arriving back in Phoenix.

Ivy unlocked the door and walked back into her cabin with Cheshire yowling in the kitty-crate three days before the big holiday weekend. The summer heat had not subsided, and people continued to throng to Lake of the Ozarks' cool waters. It would be the last big hurrah before children returned to school and the summer tourist season officially ended.

After their first night together, Dan had all but taken up residence in the cabin with Ivy. When he began parking his big rig next to the cabin, Peggy stopped and demanded to know what was going on between them.

Ivy and Dan had been planting fall tulip bulbs along the stone walkway in front of the cabin one afternoon when Peggy's pickup skidded into the drive and the woman, wearing overalls and a sweaty t-shirt, stormed out.

"Dan Wingate," Peggy stormed, "what do you think you're doing cavorting about with this horrible, godless woman," she pointed an accusatory finger at Ivy, who knelt with her hands full of soil and bulbs, "and living with her in sin under your sweet dead wife's very own roof. People in town are talking. You should be ashamed of making such a fool of poor Cindy this way."

"People in town," Dan admonished, "wouldn't know or care a damned thing about it if you didn't go runnin' off at the mouth about it at that damned church." He dropped the nylon mesh bag of bulbs but hung onto the trowel he'd been digging with and rose to face the scornful Peggy. "Now you get one thing straight, Peggy Sue Martin," he pointed the digging tool at his former cousin-in-law, "I love Cindy, and I always will, but she's dead and gone now. I promised my wife on her *deathbed* that I'd go on with my life and find somebody else to love." He bent and lifted Ivy to her feet.

"Ivy Chandler is *me* getting on with *my* life. We're good together, and we want to be together." Dan brushed Ivy's hair aside and kissed her mouth passionately before turning back to a red-faced Peggy. "We don't give a good goddamn about what you or anybody else in this town thinks about it." Dan pitched the trowel, and it landed spade-tip down in the yard at Peggy's feet. "Now, do us all a favor and get your lard-ass back in your damned truck and stop bothering us with your holier-than-thou bullshit."

"You're gonna burn in Hell, Dan Wingate, along with your filthy, godless slut." Peggy stomped on the trowel, bending its blade in the hard soil of the yard, before storming back to her pickup, throwing gravel as she spun her tires backing out.

In her haste to get out of their driveway and onto the road, Peggy miscalculated, and rather than turning out onto the narrow gravel lane, she went straight across it and backward into the deep ditch on the other side. They heard her scream as the rear end of the truck fell off into the deep drainage ditch, leaving the front end sticking straight up with the wheels spinning in mid-air.

Ivy and Dan both ran across the gravel road to see if the woman was injured but heard Peggy cursing into her cell phone at her husband on the other end, demanding that he come with the backhoe to get her and the pickup out of the ditch.

"She's fine," Dan said as he took Ivy's hand, and they returned to their bulbs. Dan straightened the bent trowel, and while Peggy's husband and son pulled her and her truck from the ditch, they finished burying the remainder of their tulip bulbs along the path. Ivy looked forward to seeing them bloom in the spring but knew every time she looked at them, she'd think of those pickup wheels spinning and laugh.

Ivy found that she and Dan made a good match. They'd both been raised on small farms and had four siblings. They'd both gone to junior colleges and married young. Dan's marriage to Cindy had lasted thirty years while Ivy had been married for thirty-four years, but to three different husbands.

They enjoyed one another's company both in and out of the bedroom. Dan told her about how Cindy had loved to garden and how he'd loved getting the ground ready for her to plant. He'd sold all his gardening equipment but assured Ivy they could get more in the spring. When Ivy had asked him about the chicken coop, he'd curled his lip in distaste.

"I hated those damned birds, but Cindy insisted on 'em. When new ones hatched, she'd bring the little bastards into the house and baby 'em for weeks until they were big enough to go out into the pullet cage where she warmed 'em with a heat lamp if it was still cold at night." He shook his head. "I used to ask her how she thought the mommas took care of 'em before electricity, and she'd just snarl at me like I was an uncaring ass or something." He stared at Ivy for reinforcement. "I mean, who brings nasty-assed chickens into their house?"

"My mom always did," Ivy told him. "She said the snakes or rats would get them if she didn't. If we didn't have hens or they weren't laying, we went without eggs."

Ivy watched Dan stare off into space for a minute. "Now that you mention it, neither did we. Mom made biscuits and gravy when we didn't have eggs." He smiled at Ivy. "But she never brought the damned chicks into the living room and kept 'em in a box smellin' the place up either. My old man would've had a flippin' cow."

She and Dan spent hours talking about their childhoods and young adulthoods. Ivy could not believe the difference between the way Dan made her feel compared to the way Carl had. There was no stress or self-doubt with Dan. He treated her like an equal, and Ivy finally realized the thing missing between her and Carl. He couldn't see her as an equal. To Carl, Ivy would always be beneath him, and he made her feel that way. Perhaps he hadn't intended to make her feel that way, but Ivy finally saw that he had.

Dan gave her an easy, contented feeling, and Ivy was completely comfortable with him. Giving it some consideration, Ivy found that contentment to be more important than anything Carl had ever had to offer. The sex had been great, but there was so much more to a relationship than great sex. She and Dan had really great sex, but they also had great conversations, laughter, and common interests.

Ivy carried the last of her boxes into the cabin, shut the door, and freed Cheshire from the confines of his crate. Cheshire had been an indoor cat since Ivy found him as a kitten. In the car, she'd kept him in the crate and put him on a leash to take him out to do his business as they traveled. Ivy had laughed at his confusion the first few times he'd realized he was supposed to do his thing in the grass and not in his cozy box of sand. He held it for a while but finally figured things out and resigned himself to going in the grass at rest areas. Ivy was glad he'd never messed inside the crate while they traveled in her new car.

When she filled his box with litter and put it in the utility room next to the washer, Cheshire jumped into it with joy and relieved himself in one long steady stream. Ivy could almost see the contentment on his broad orange face as he scratched at the sandy litter in the plastic box. After jumping from the box, he found his food and water dishes in the kitchen and ate heartily. Ivy was glad to have him here so he could get back on a regular schedule. She watched him explore his new surroundings, jumping up onto the furniture and sniffing everything.

"This is home now, buddy. Momma promises not to drag you around anymore for a long time." Ivy sat on the couch, and Cheshire joined her, nudging her hand with his nose for petting. The big yellow tabby purred when she obliged and curled up next to Ivy to fall asleep. She continued to run her hands through his thick fur. "I'm sorry, buddy. You must be exhausted after that trip." She sat with him for a while before she finally rose to attend to all the things piled by the front door.

Ivy carried her suitcases into her bedroom and threw them onto the bed. She would empty them after everything else was put away. Ivy emptied the totes of pots and pans into cabinets in the kitchen. She found a spot for her microwave and placed a decorative glass dish atop it, so it didn't look so stark and modern in the country kitchen. Her blender and toaster she stored in the pantry to be taken out when needed. Ivy's collection of heavy stoneware mixing bowls went atop the upper cabinets. She left her favorite one down for everyday use.

Finishing the kitchen, the only items left were her two flat-screen televisions. After moving into the cabin, Ivy had called DirectTV and had a satellite dish installed and the living room and two bedrooms wired for the televisions. Dan had brought a small television over for them to use in their bedroom until she could bring her own back from Phoenix.

Ivy could have simply bought new ones and left the others in storage with her things, but she feared the delicate electronics would get broken, and they weren't that old. She put one on a table in the living room and the other in her bedroom. They'd already decided Dan's little one would go into the guest room for her grandsons to use when visiting, so Ivy carried it in and sat it atop the dresser.

With everything put away except her clothes, Ivy made a sandwich and dropped onto the couch to relax and watch some television. Cheshire rose and nudged her hand for a bite of turkey from her sandwich. Ivy jumped when a loud crack of thunder interrupted the silence. She leaped up from the couch to look outside to be sure she'd closed all the windows and shut the doors and trunk of the car. Rain began to spatter on the asphalt road in front of the cabin. The car was, indeed, shut up tight, and Ivy returned to her sandwich to find only bread on the plate and Cheshire licking mayo from his face and paws.

"You're a bad kitty," Ivy scolded and took her plate back into the kitchen to replace the pilfered turkey slices. Thunder rattled the windows again, and Ivy could see the tops of the tall trees twisting in the wind as bright lightning shot across the darkened sky. Ivy enjoyed the sound of the rain on the cabin's metal roof, but she hoped she wouldn't hear hail as well. Dan had promised to build her a carport, but for now, her shiny new Lexus sat at the mercy of Mother Nature.

Ivy returned to the couch with her reassembled sandwich to catch the blare of the severe weather warning. She was relieved to see only a severe thunderstorm advisory and not a tornado warning. One tornado that year had proven to be more than enough for Ivy Chandler. She could tell the wind was picking up and wondered if she should bring in her wicker from the porch. Not wanting to go searching for it tomorrow blown across the countryside, Ivy stepped out onto the porch. To her great relief, the wind blew from behind the cabin. She scooted the chairs away from the edge of the porch and collected the cushion from the swing so it wouldn't get soaked by the blowing rain.

As she dumped the cushion onto the floor in front of the fireplace, she wondered where Dan was tonight. He'd told her he would try to be home before the weekend when she'd called to let him know she was on her way back from Arizona. Cheshire pounced upon the cushion and looked up at Ivy as if to ask permission but curled up tightly on the thick, soft cushion before she could give it. Ivy shook her head and clicked through channels until she found something interesting.

Her phone chimed, and Ivy answered. "Hello, Ivy Chandler."

"Hi, Ivy, it's Dan."

"Hi," she said, relieved to hear his voice. "Where are you, sweetie?"

"Still in Georgia," he huffed. "Dispatch was supposed to have a load for me today, but I'm here still waiting. It looks like I might be stuck here until after the damned weekend," he said with a deep sigh. "I'm sorry."

"That's alright. I have some revisions to get done for my editor." Ivy jumped with another clap of thunder and almost dropped the phone. "How's the weather there? It's raining cats and dogs here."

"You're home then?" he asked, and Ivy could hear the relief in his voice.

"Yes, just got in this afternoon. I even got the car unloaded and everything put away before the rain hit."

"That's good. How's the cat?" Dan hadn't been thrilled about the prospect of having a cat inside the house, and Ivy appreciated his thoughtfulness in asking about him.

"He's curled up on the swing cushion in front of the fireplace."

"Making himself at home then? That's good." Dan chuckled. "There are storm warnings here, too. It seems a hurricane has kicked up in the Atlantic that might make landfall close to here sometime tonight."

"That's just great," Ivy sighed. "I went through a tornado and now you a hurricane. Do we attract bad weather or something?"

"I called my dispatcher and told her that if things get hairy here, I'm headin' home." He sounded worried.

"How bad is it?" she asked, worry now creeping into her voice.

"Stormin' pretty bad right now, and the weather station says they may evacuate the county. I'm parked on high ground here, but if it rains much more, the roads may flood in the lower-lying areas. I just don't know how much longer I should wait it out."

"Just come on home then," Ivy urged. "You can pick up a load from here. I haven't seen you in weeks."

"It's only been two weeks, and you were on the road, too."

"I know, but I miss you." Ivy looked up to see the path of the hurricane being flashed on the weather channel. "That hurricane is making landfall now on the Georgia-Florida border according to what I'm seeing on the Weather Channel."

"Yeah, I'm out of here. They just announced that the county is being evacuated. I'm in the coffee shop at the truck stop, and they just blasted it on the PA system. I gotta go."

"OK, sweetie. Be safe and call or text me later. I'll keep my phone close."

"I will. Ivy?"

"Yes?"

"I love you," he said quickly. "I gotta fly, woman. Talk to ya later." He disconnected before Ivy could reply to his announcement.

Ivy sat with the phone in her hand, staring at the blank screen. His words repeated in her head. *Ivy? I love you.* Her heart fluttered in her chest, and her belly churned. Tears sprang to her eyes. No man had said those words to her and sounded like he meant it in years. Ivy closed her eyes tight.

Why didn't I say it back before he hung up? Was he waiting for me to say it back? I couldn't say it back. He hung up too quickly. Should I call him back? No, he's trying to get the truck ready to roll in a storm. I'll wait.

Self-doubt plagued Ivy for the next two hours. She tucked her phone in the pocket of her robe, and she willed it to ring, but it didn't. She started to punch in his number a dozen times but didn't want to bother him while he drove, especially in bad weather.

Ivy sat on the couch, sipping hot chocolate and watching the Weather Channel. She tangled her fingers in her brunette bob and reached for her phone again. It chimed, and Ivy fumbled to open and answer it.

"Hello," she said anxiously.

"Hi, baby," Carl replied in a flippant tone, and Ivy wanted to end the call in frustration. "How are you doing out there in the sticks in this weather tonight?"

"We're fine," Ivy replied flatly.

"You and trucker boy?" Carl asked with a sneer.

"No, Cheshire and I. Dan's on the road." Hearing his name, Cheshire uncurled from his cushion and stretched.

"You went back to Phoenix already?" Carl asked with surprise.

"Just got back this afternoon. You haven't gone back yet?"

"No, I'm still here. I wanted to get everything all set with the condos before I drove back."

"Judith's not going to fly out and pick you up?" Ivy asked in a catty tone.

"We talked about it," Carl said with some hesitation, "but she's got business out there until the end of the month."

"What is it between the two of you, really?" Ivy asked but didn't know if she wanted him to be truthful or not.

"Judith and I have been intimate friends since before the divorce from her last husband."

Finally, the truth. Much more than just friends and business associates.

"She's a beautiful woman," Ivy admitted. "She looks good on your arm."

"Now, don't be that way, baby. You knew I was seeing other women. You saw other men. We were never exclusive."

"I know that, Carl," Ivy paused, "and now we're nothing at all."

"Oh come on, baby. Wouldn't you like to have a warm body next to you in that atrocious bedroom on a stormy night like tonight?" Carl chuckled but sounded hopeful.

"I'd love to have a warm body in my bed tonight," Ivy sighed, "but not yours." She gave that a second to sink in. "Why did Judith light out of here so quickly after seeing me?"

"It wasn't seeing *you* exactly." He sounded like he wanted to say more.

"Then what *exactly* was it?" Ivy prodded.

"She said she didn't like the way I reacted when I saw you leaving Powell's office with that Dan guy hanging all over you."

"Dan said she had the look of a woman who thought she was more than just a business associate."

"Yeah, I guess she does," Carl sighed. "She seemed to think that trip out here was going to be more than just business, and when she saw you here signing papers on the same day we were, she thought you and I had arranged it that way." Ivy thought Carl sounded genuinely upset about Judith's reaction.

"So, she knew about me?"

"She knew about our trip out here." He paused. "She saw us on the news after the tornado."

"Like I saw you two in the paper in Phoenix?" Ivy couldn't help rubbing salt into the wound.

"Something like that," he admitted.

"And she never thought you two *didn't* have an exclusive relationship?"

"It's different with Judith, baby. I need her for the business. Her development company underwrites most of my deals."

"Having a woman with money on the side is handy, I suppose."

"And trucker boy doesn't see you as a big bank account now that your rolling in dough from your book deal? How does it feel to be the one being used for a change?" Carl sneered.

"As a matter of fact," Ivy fumed, "he does not see me as a cash-cow in any way. He makes a good living with his truck and has no need of my paltry funds.

Carl, I never asked you for a damned thing in the entire year we saw one another."

"You may not have asked outright, but you certainly implied plenty."

"I'm really sorry you saw it that way, Carl. Good luck with the condos and with Judith." Ivy hung up.

18

Like most of the locals, Ivy avoided the lake and the main drag in Branson over the Labor Day weekend. She spent her holiday on her porch swing with her laptop on her knees, making the revisions to her manuscript the editor wanted. She couldn't understand why they were in such a big hurry for it. The contract said they had eighteen months to publish.

Dan hadn't made it back yet. He'd gotten away from the storm, but his dispatcher had found him a load to pick up in Texas to haul up to St. Louis. He took it, and Ivy expected him back soon.

After her conversation with Carl, Ivy had driven by the condo with the boat slip and saw him tying a sporty go-fast boat to the dock. She wondered if Judith Merriman was underwriting that purchase too. It gave Ivy some satisfaction to hear Carl admit what she'd always suspected he thought of her. It broke her heart, but she was glad to know it. Her self-doubt hadn't been unfounded after all.

Dan had called a few minutes after she'd hung up with Carl, and when she'd answered, Ivy had thought it might be her ex-lover calling back.

"What?" Ivy snapped.

"Am I interrupting you or something?" Dan asked at her abrupt greeting.

"Oh no, sweetie," Ivy apologized. "I thought it was someone else."

"Now who'd be calling my woman this late and upsetting her?"

"It was Carl," she said with a sigh. "He finally admitted that he thought I was just after him for his money."

"I thought it was the blonde who has the money."

"Yes, but I couldn't have known that when we met," Ivy chirped, "and she left him here because she thought he and I had set something up behind her back."

"Not like he didn't try."

"He was still trying tonight." Ivy laughed. "Can you believe that?"

"What did the son-of-a-bitch say?" Dan asked angrily. "He's got a lot of nerve trying to bed my woman when he knows she's already taken."

"Yes, and *after* he insulted my bedroom decor."

"Pretty ballsy guy. You might get by with snakin' another man's woman, but you'll never get lucky insulting her decorating." Dan laughed, and Ivy joined him.

"I am. You know." Ivy told him.

"You are what?"

"I *am* your woman." Ivy took a deep breath before finishing. "I love you too, Dan Wingate, and I'm happy to call myself your woman."

"I know that," he said softly through the phone into her ear. "I've known it since our first night together. A woman doesn't do a man like you done me unless there's the possibility of some love there. And

I love you. I never thought there'd be another woman for me after my Cindy." He paused, and Ivy checked to see if she'd lost the connection. "I screwed a few but I could never love any of 'em. You're a special woman, Ivy Chandler, and I'm proud to say I love you."

"And I'm proud to say I love you, too, Danny." Ivy sighed a mental sigh of relief. "How's the weather where you are now?"

"I ran out of the storm about an hour ago, and I'm gonna pull into the next stop for the night and let my dispatcher know what's up in the morning."

"That's good. Call me in the morning too. The worst of the storm's passed through here, too, and it's just a light rain now."

"Maybe the town will get its last hurrah for the summer after all. Goodnight, Ivy. I love you, and I'll call you in the mornin'." Again, he cut her off before she could respond. She was going to have to talk to him about that.

Ivy got a warm feeling all over every time she reran that conversation in her head.

He loves me. He's handsome, he respects me, and he loves me. What more could a woman possibly want?

The next day, as Ivy sat in her swing, pondering that, Peggy drove by. Children in swimming suits, holding inflated beach toys, filled the rear of her slightly crumpled pick up. Ivy waved. The laughing children waved back and yelled greetings, but Peggy turned her head away. Ivy shook hers and went back to the work on her laptop.

Dusk fell, and Dan still had not returned. Ivy blamed it on the holiday traffic and wondered if his delivery point would even be manned over the holiday weekend. She hoped he wouldn't be stuck in St. Louis until Tuesday when businesses reopened. The mosquitoes were still active and had begun to plague her. She rousted Cheshire from the cushion beside her, and they went inside.

Ivy had begun taking the cat outside with her the day after their return. She wanted Cheshire to become familiar with his new home. The first few forays, he'd stayed close to her side, but after a few days, he'd jumped from the porch to explore the yard and chase butterflies and bumblebees in the clover.

Ivy enjoyed watching the cat discover things for the first time. She watched him closely, though, because she'd seen several giant black snakes out on the road and didn't want him to try playing with one of those. He would never be allowed outside at night as Ivy had heard coyotes yipping in the distance many nights since moving into the rural cabin.

The rattling engine of Dan's big rig woke Ivy around three as he parked in the gravel area he'd made for the big truck beside the cabin after making certain Ivy welcomed his company there. She rose and met him at the door with open arms.

"I'm glad you're home." She let him wrap her in a tight bear hug.

"That sounds nice, you know," he whisper into her ear.

"What?" She tilted her head back to look his big hazel eyes.

"Home," he sighed. "It's nice to hear you call this my home."

"Our home." Ivy kissed him and melted into his strong embrace.

Dan flipped the switch to turn off the porch light, took Ivy's hand, and led her into the bedroom.

"What exactly does that ballsy old bastard think is wrong with this bedroom?" Dan asked as he reached in and turned on the light in the bathroom.

The blue glow from the television screen illuminated the brass bed and the soft, girly room.

"It's all the shabby chic painted furniture," Ivy explained. "People who are really into antiques think it ruins the value of a piece of furniture to paint it and decorate it with stencils and such."

"Well, that's just bullshit," Dan huffed. "Cindy did it with pieces that were junk otherwise with stained or ruined finishes. She picked up pieces at yard sales and second-hand stores all the time. She'd paint 'em up and sell 'em to that old reprobate Humphry for a good profit. People like it, and this room looks really pretty the way you have it fixed it up."

"Thanks, Danny. You're so sweet."

Ivy had begun calling him Danny during love-making, and it had stuck during their private moments together. He'd asked her not to call him by that name in public as it had been his moniker in childhood and had taken him years to get his friends and family to use the more adult Dan.

"I need a shower. You want to join me?" He taunted her by stripping off his sweaty t-shirt to reveal his toned, muscular upper body and tanned arms.

Damn, he looks good for a sixty-year-old man. He has a little gray in his hair and the beginnings of a very slight paunch at his mid-section, but the rest of him still looks fine. Not a soft spot on that man.

Ivy fell back into the bed. "I had one before bed. I'll wait for you here." She blew him a kiss.

"Your loss," he teased and let his jeans fall to the floor, exposing the large bulge in his tighty-whities.

Ivy pulled off her long sleep shirt and stretched nude upon the pink sheets. "I've waited this long." She raised her right knee and let it fall over to expose her vagina. "I think I can wait for another ten minutes." Ivy moved her hand and began massaging her swelling clit. "I'll get her all ready for you."

Dan stood silhouetted in the doorway open-mouthed. "You're an evil woman, Ivy Chandler."

She watched him peel off the white underpants and laughed. "So cousin Peggy says. I'm an evil, godless woman living in sin and shameless." Ivy heard the water begin running in the shower and the glass door slide shut. She made herself comfortable upon the pillows and switched the channel on the television. She found a creature feature on SYFY and waited for Dan to finish his shower.

Ivy must have fallen asleep because Dan woke her when he flopped his damp body onto the bed, burying his cool, stubbled face between her breasts. His hand found its way to her crotch and probed.

"Is she ready for action, or is she asleep too?" Dan laughed as he bit at a nipple. It hardened with his attention. "That's awake." He pinched the other, rolling it roughly between his thumb and forefinger. "That one's awake, too." He knew what she liked and pinched harder, pulling the nipple into his mouth between his teeth and biting.

Ivy, her clit beginning to throb with his attention to her nipples, could feel his stiff erection sliding against her thigh. She reached down and grasped his balls. "He's awake." Ivy gasped as Dan bit harder but trailed a fingertip from his balls up the hefty shaft to circle the bulging head lightly. She rested it on the tender spot just under the spout.

"Oh, woman," he moaned and loosed her nipple from his mouth. "You keep that up, and I'm gonna cum all over your leg."

"You'd better not do that. I just changed these sheets today." Ivy spread her legs wider, and he climbed atop her waiting body. Dan eased himself into her the way she liked, popping the head in and out a few times before going all the way in and slapping her ass cheeks with his heavy balls.

"Oh, yeah, Danny," Ivy moaned, "just like that." She let out a loud groan when he finally shoved into her and kept up a strong, steady rhythm while she arched up to meet his eager thrusts.

"I'm not gonna last long tonight," he panted as he pinched her nipple to bring on her release. As her pulsing orgasm clasped his erection, Dan groaned out a loud, "Fucking Christ, woman."

Ivy pulled his face down to hers and kissed him, quieting him. "Not so loud, Danny. If Peggy hears that, she'll have us both burned at the stake as blasphemers."

"She doesn't live that close," Dan chided as he rolled off to lie panting by Ivy's side. "And I'm not *that* loud."

"Yes, you are." Ivy pulled tissues from the box by the bed and stuffed them into her weeping vagina. "And the windows are open."

"Her house is a half-mile up the road."

"I know, and like I said, the windows are open. Sound travels up this hollow. I hear her yelling at those grandkids all the time."

Dan laughed, went into the bathroom to wipe off, and flipped off the light before returning to the bed. *Their bed.* Ivy smiled, listening to the sounds of the night coming in past the lace curtains, being moved about by a gentle, cool breeze. Crickets and katydids chirped, whippoorwills cooed, and coyotes yipped in the distance. The lowing of a cow registered in Ivy's head along with the gentle snores of Dan beside her as she drifted off to sleep in the early morning hours of Labor Day.

19

Ivy woke to the aroma of coffee. She sat up, stretched, and pulled on her long t-shirt. After a quick stop in the bathroom, she shuffled into the kitchen, where Dan stood over the stove, cracking eggs into a skillet. She went to the cabinet and took down cups.

"Smells great in here." Ivy stood on her tiptoes and kissed Dan on his stubbled cheek. "Who taught you to cook?"

"My mom. She always said a man needed to know how to take care of himself, so we learned how to cook and do laundry just like the girls."

"Smart woman." Ivy poured them both some coffee after checking to make sure Dan hadn't poured one for himself already. "You want your coffee over there?"

"No, just put it on the table. I'm about done over here." He walked to the table with the skillet and scraped cheesy scrambled eggs onto their plates.

Ivy reached over and gave his firm backside a swat. "I'm so glad you're home."

Dan took the skillet to the sink and filled it with

water. Back at the table, he took Ivy's hand and kissed it. "Me too."

Cheshire, generally shy with new people at first, avoided Dan, but the smell of food and Ivy's presence lured the cat into the kitchen. He rubbed up against Ivy's leg and twined his sinewy body around her ankles. Ivy scooted her chair back and picked up the cat. "Dan, this is Cheshire Sandwich-thief."

Dan reached over, petted the purring feline, and offered him a bite of the savory, cheesy eggs. Cheshire sniffed at it before snatching it from Dan's fingers. "Hello, Cheshire. We'll be friends, but if you try snakin' my sandwiches, I'll probably boot your furry ass off the porch." Dan rubbed his hands on his jeans before returning to his food.

Ivy dropped the cat to the floor, used a paper towel to wipe her hands, and picked up her fork.

"These eggs are great. Your mom did a good job."

"They're much better when you use Velveeta, but all you had were Kraft Singles. These were actually my dad's specialty." Dan took a big bite, followed by a drink of coffee. "He made breakfast every Sunday morning to give my mom a break."

"I promise to remember Velveeta the next time I stop in at the IGA if you promise me more Sunday breakfasts like this." Ivy laughed.

"Only if you promise *me* Saturday nights like last night." He grinned and held out his right hand for a shake.

Ivy took his hand. "Deal."

They finished their breakfast, chatting about their plans for the next week. Dan needed to take the big truck in for a new tire and wanted to get the lumber to build the carport next to the cabin.

"What would you think about extending the deck

on around the end of the cabin to connect to the carport? Cindy showed me a picture in a magazine once that had a deck like that, and we always talked about building one, bu—" His face clouded a little.

"That sounds great, Dan. Cindy had great taste, and if she thought it would look good, I'm all for it. What would you think about a hot tub?" Ivy offered tentatively.

He looked at her and smiled. "We could put it in the spot where the porch turns the corner. Then we could get to it from the front door or the back."

"Wonderful. A hot tub would be great in the cooler weather. I love to soak in hot water."

"Me too, but would you want it right out front where anybody driving by could see?" Ivy knew he meant Peggy and her nosy friends.

"Good point. Why don't we build the deck all the way down to the rear edge of the house beyond the carport and put the tub back there. We'd be restricted to using the back door, but that's alright."

"Great." Dan grabbed a pen from the counter and a paper towel. He made a rough sketch of the planned deck and carport with the hot tub at the rear. "I'll put a lattice cover over the tub to keep out the worst of the leaves in the fall and shade it a little in the summer."

"We could plant a flowering vine to grow up over it or maybe some grapes," Ivy added with an enthusiastic smile.

"That might defeat the purpose if we end up with leaves and dead flowers floating around in the water anyway." Dan laughed.

Their discussion was interrupted by a loud knock at the front door. Ivy heard a vehicle driving away but couldn't get a good look at it by the time she got to the door. She looked down to see a basket with a wicker handle. A red gingham cloth covered the contents. Ivy picked it up and carried it back into the kitchen.

"Someone left us a gift." Ivy set the basket on the table and lifted off the cloth. The scent of spicy muffins wafted up into her nose. "There's a note." Ivy opened the little piece of paper folded and tied to the side of the handle with a red ribbon.

Welcome, New Neighbor,

Please accept this small token of welcome. We hope you will feel free to join us for services on Sundays.

Your friends at The Mount Pleasant Methodist Church.

"Isn't this sweet," Ivy said and picked up one of the big, heavy muffins. She put it to her nose and inhaled. "Zucchini, I think. I hope they have walnuts. Shall we have one with the rest of our coffee out on the porch?"

"I'm stuffed." Dan rubbed his belly but picked up his cup and refilled it. "But sitting outside sounds nice." He followed Ivy out onto the porch to sit in one of the cushioned wicker chairs. "Enjoy your muffin. I'll have one later."

Ivy bit into the moist muffin. "Umm," she moaned with pleasure as she chewed. "Walnuts *and* raisins. This is divine. Don't let me forget to send them a nice thank-you note."

Dan grimaced as he watched her devour the muffin followed by coffee. "Am I your secretary now, Ms. Chandler?" He finally broke into a smile, watching her finish the muffin, picking crumbs from her lap and popping them into her mouth. He stood.

"I don't know where you're gonna put it, but I'll get you another." He walked into the cabin and returned with another heavy, moist muffin in one hand and a fresh pot of coffee in the other. "You're gonna get fat if you eat all those muffins. Why don't you put a few of them in a Ziploc and throw them into the freezer." He refilled Ivy's cup and set the pot onto the table.

The muffin spiced with cinnamon, cloves, and nutmeg filled her mouth and delighted Ivy. She crunched into a nut and chewed a sweet raisin.

This is the perfect combination for a muffin. I'm going to have to beg the baker for her recipe.

When they finally emptied the pot of coffee, Dan suggested they run into the nearest town with a Home Depot to price the lumber for the porch and carport.

"Wouldn't it be better to buy local? Is there a building supply store here in town?" Ivy asked as she picked up their cups and the coffee pot.

"Yeah, but their stock of inventory isn't good, and they're pretty pricey."

"I'd rather spend my money locally if you don't mind," Ivy said. "Those big-box stores have put so many little local vendors out of business."

"It's your money, Ms. Chandler. You're more than welcome to spend it where you like," Dan said in his exaggerated Southern accent.

"Don't patronize me, Danny," Ivy chided. "I have several old friends back home whose parents went bankrupt after Wal-Mart came into our little town, undercut their prices, stole their employees, and drove them out of business. I'll always shop local in a small town, especially if it's *my* small town."

"Guess I can't argue with that. I don't know if the local lumber yard is open today, but we can check it out."

Ivy finished the dishes with Dan pestering her, slapping her behind and nibbling on her neck every time he passed. It had been a long time since Ivy had someone to play slap and tickle with while she tried to work. She found it distracting but enjoyable.

The local lumber yard was open for business, to Dan's dismay, and quite busy. The aroma of new-cut lumber filled Ivy's nose as they walked in, and Ivy took a deep breath. She loved that smell. One of her former husbands had teased Ivy that if he wanted to get a little, all he had to do was take her to the Home Depot because she always left horny after shopping. Ivy wasn't certain that was true, but she *did* enjoy home design and shopping for paint, wallpaper, and trims.

She related that story to Dan, and he gave her a lascivious smile. "I'll test that out, and if it's true, we'll have to make this a regular thing."

"Yeah, right." She gave him a playful swat on the shoulder. "The cabin is perfect the way it is. I don't need new paint, wallpaper, or cabinets." Ivy furrowed her brow in thought. "I would like to look at cabinet pulls, though. I want to get some round white porcelain ones to match the ones on the pie safe."

"You see," he chuckled, "I knew there would be something. I was married to the queen of home design for thirty years. I'd come here for one thing, and if I brought Cindy along, we'd leave with the truck loaded fully."

"How are you at plumbing?" Ivy giggled. "I'd like to change out the faucets for those black Victorian-looking ones to match the towel bars."

Dan rolled his eyes as he followed Ivy to the

plumbing department, where she stopped in front of a display of faucets and showerheads. "Aren't these cool?" Ivy asked as she picked up a black shower head nine inches wide with bright brass fittings that set off the dull black finish. She pointed to a sizeable goose-neck sink faucet as well. "These are perfect."

Ivy was laughing when she suddenly doubled over in gut-wrenching pain and vomited onto the floor of the wide plumbing aisle. "Oh, my God, Danny." She grasped his arm for support. "I'm so dizzy… I think I'm gonna pass out." Ivy's stomach heaved again, and she felt the bile coming up her throat. She took a breath but began choking.

"Honey, what's wrong?" she heard Danny asking, but his voice sounded so far away. He slapped her back as she tried to clear her throat of the suffocating vomit. Her body began to shake. She had no control. "Ivy… Ivy." Then she didn't see Dan's face or the plumbing aisle any longer. Everything went black.

20

Ivy lost track of time. She thought she saw Dan's face or heard his voice a few times. People she didn't know asked her questions she couldn't answer. Carrie was there holding her hand for a time. People tried to make her sit up. She couldn't stay up. She fell over onto her side. Ivy just wanted to sleep. Why wouldn't these people let her sleep? She pushed someone away and then drifted off.

Dappled spring sunlight drifted down through the leaves of the big maple tree in her grandparents' yard. Ivy looked up to see her grandpa sitting on his porch swing, a cigarette hanging from the side of his mouth. He sorted strawberries into quart boxes that would fit twelve quarts per cardboard flat.

"Ivy girl, what are you doing here? You're too early. You need to go back." He continued to sort the berries for that day's sales from the little stand he and her younger brothers had built by the edge of the drive. Ivy was confused.

Why would he want me to go back home? We live ten miles away, and I just got here. I'm supposed to pick berries today. Why would he want me to go back?

"I came to get an early start while it's still cool, Grandpa."

"No, you're too early, you need to go back." He blew smoke from around the cigarette clamped in his lips. "Go on back now, Ivy girl." The burning cigarette bounced up and down between his lips as he spoke.

"Where's Granny?" Ivy asked. Granny would understand.

"She's in the house." Her grandpa pointed toward the front door of the bungalow built for her grandfather by his grandfather, the house her mother had been raised in, and the house where Ivy's parents had lived when she'd been born. Now her grandparents lived here again, having moved back from town some years ago.

Ivy went to the door and twisted the big brass knob. It confused her that she found the door locked. Ivy twisted the knob again to no avail and then knocked. She soon saw her grandmother's perfectly coifed red hair appear on the other side of the thick glass in the craftsman-style door. "It's Ivy, Granny. Let me in."

"Iva Leigh, you are here much too soon. You must go back." Ivy saw a bright light coming from behind her grandmother. That confused Ivy even more. Granny never had the kitchen light on during the day, saying it used too much electricity. The light was so bright, so warm and inviting. Ivy wanted to see where it was coming from. She'd never seen the light so bright shining in Granny's kitchen. It added to her confusion.

Ivy twisted the knob and pushed on the door. To her surprise, it wasn't locked anymore, but her grandmother leaned against it, denying Ivy entry. "Go back, Iva Leigh," Granny said in that stern voice Ivy didn't dare to disobey. "It's too soon for you to be here. Go on back now."

Ivy blinked fast to ward off tears but backed away from the door, as she'd been told. She turned to wave at her grandpa. "You go on back for now, Ivy girl, and I promise we'll be here waiting when it's really time for ya to come back." Ivy didn't understand but she did as her grandparents insisted and walked back down the stairs and into the deep, cool shade of the big maple tree.

21

The loud, angry voices of men arguing woke her. Ivy thought she should know the men talking, but she felt so fuzzy-headed. She couldn't understand what was going on. A minute ago, she'd stood at her grandparent's house, getting ready to pick strawberries. Now she lay in a strange bed. Ivy tried to talk but choked. A plastic tube filled her mouth and ran down her throat. Aside from the loud voices of the men, Ivy heard the beeping and chiming of machines. She tried to sit up. She needed to pee.

"This is your damned fault," one man yelled.

Ivy stopped trying to move and listened to the shouting men. She knew down deep that she should know who they were, but the names simply wouldn't come to her.

"How to hell is it my fault that somebody sent her poisoned muffins?"

"It's obviously someone from here who is pissed that you're living with Ivy in that house where you once lived with your dead wife. One of these crazy hillbilly religious nuts probably took offense and poisoned her."

"And what about your jealous, rich-bitch girlfriend, who wanted Ivy out of the way?"

"Judith has no idea where Ivy lives. She wouldn't know about local churches anyhow."

"Mister, she's rich. She could pay somebody to come out here and find out about that sort of thing. I saw the way she looked at Ivy in Powell's office. If looks could kill, Ivy would have been dead then and there. I know crazy when I see it, and that blonde had crazy written all over her damned face." The voice stopped to draw breath before continuing. "You put crazy and rich together, and you've got trouble. Have the police talked to you yet? I talked to them already and told 'em about your crazy blonde girlfriend."

"I guarantee you, Judith Merriman has nothing to do with this. It was probably one of those crazy bitches I heard talking in the diner last week. They were saying terrible things about Ivy and you. They think the two of you have shamed your poor dead wife and were going on about the wrath of God raining down upon the two of you. If you ask me, Mr. Wingate, that's the crazy the police should be looking into."

Ivy tried to move again. Monitors began to blare, and Ivy heard the rubber soles of shoes running into the room. Ivy opened her eyes. A woman wearing a ridiculous Hello Kitty smock bent over her while a young man in a plain blue smock pushed buttons on the blaring machine next to her bed.

"Well, it's good to see you're finally awake, Ms. Chandler. We've been waiting for a good while now."

Ivy tried to speak. "Don't try to talk, Ms. Chandler. We put a tube down your throat to help you breathe." She looked at the monitor. "Your sats look good. I'll call the doctor, and maybe we can get that tube out of your mouth so you can talk." The nurse walked away and was replaced by the two men Ivy had heard arguing. Each walked to either side of the bed and took a hand. Her eyes darted between the two. She should know them.

"Hi, baby," the man with white hair said. "How are you feeling? You gave us all quite a scare."

Ivy tried to smile at his courtesy but could not. She wanted to ask questions, and she really wanted to pee.

"Hey, honey," the bigger man with brown curly hair said. His hazel eyes looked worried with dark circles beneath them. "You're gonna be alright now. The doc said that if you woke up by tonight, you'd be alright." He ran a hand over her head and gently pushed a lock of matted hair behind her ear. "Cheshire is alright, but he misses you. He just sits out on the porch swing waiting for you."

The vision of a fat yellow tabby cat flashed into Ivy's head, and she wanted to smile. As other hospital employees came and went, Ivy's head cleared, and she regained more memories. The white-haired man's name was Carl, and the other was Danny. When those names came back to her, tears slid down her cheeks.

What in hell's name is going on? What were they talking about? Poisoned muffins? Why are they both here? Dan should be here. But why is Carl? He thinks I'm a gold digger. God, I need to pee.

A tall, thin black man wearing a white lab coat came into the room carrying a metal clipboard. He leafed through the papers before looking at the numbers on the machines beeping and clicking by her bed before speaking to her.

"Your numbers look good, Ms. Chandler, so we're going to take you off the ventilator now. He flipped a button, and the wheezing machine stopped pumping air into Ivy's lungs. "I'm going to pull this tube out. When I say 'now,' I want you to exhale as hard as you can." He took hold of the white plastic tube. "Now," he said and yanked the tube from Ivy's throat.

Ivy exhaled, but it hurt, and she ended up coughing and choking. It passed quickly, though, and Ivy got more flashes of memory. She had choked on her own vomit and rolled in the aisle of a store that smelled like fresh-cut lumber and vomit. Strong hands had held her and slapped Ivy's back.

She settled back into the pillows and tried to take short, easy breaths. Her chest hurt when she did, and she smelled and tasted vanilla pudding. How odd. Ivy tried to tell the doctor she needed to pee, but the words wouldn't form.

"Don't try to talk, ma'am, that tube had your vocal cords compressed. Your voice will come back in an hour or two. Just relax." The young doctor adjusted her blanket and put a stethoscope to her chest. "You aspirated vomit and came down with a bad case of pneumonia," the doctor explained. "You had to be intubated. Luckily, you threw up most of those poisoned muffins, or we might have lost you for good. You went into cardiac arrest at one point, and we had to use the paddles on you, but you came right back. Some fool ground up poison toadstools in that muffin batter." He shook his head. "Nasty stuff." He adjusted Ivy's pillows. "This tube in your nose is a feeding tube. And you have a catheter in. Your kidney function seems to be fine, and the output is clear. That's what we really have to worry about with those poisonous toadstools; kidney failure. We'll be taking out the catheter momentarily." He patted her leg and walked out the door.

Someone gave me poisoned muffins? Oh, my God. Who would do something like that?

Ivy remembered picking up the basket of muffins from the porch. She remembered how good they'd tasted with her coffee.

Not long after the doctor left the room, a young blonde nurse came in and removed the irritating catheter. Ivy sighed with immediate relief. She gave a long sigh like the one she gave when she'd been holding her bladder for too long and finally got to sit on the toilet and pee.

"The doctor wants to leave the feeding tube in until your throat has a chance to recover from the intubation." She winked at Ivy and smiled. "Believe me, the Ensure going in with the tube is better than the food coming out of the kitchen downstairs." She offered Ivy a cup of ice water with a straw. "Sip this slow so I can see how you swallow."

Ivy sucked some of the cold water into her mouth. It felt good on her tongue, and she swallowed slowly with no problems. The nurse pulled the straw away before Ivy was ready. "Lie back now, honey, and rest. They'll be coming in to take blood later, and your gentlemen friends are waiting outside." She winked at Ivy again. "Those two have been by your side the entire week. We had to break 'em up and put 'em in separate corners a couple of times, but they've both been plenty worried about you."

22

Dan and Carl returned to Ivy's side soon after the nurse departed her room. They both pulled chairs up close to the bed and glared at one another over her. Dan stood and took Ivy's hand, careful of the IV needle stuck in the vein there.

"How are you feelin', honey?" he asked and squeezed her hand. "Don't try to talk," he said when she opened her mouth and attempted to form a word.

Ivy felt the warmth from his hand radiating up her arm and into her heart. The other man held her hand too, but there was no warmth there. Carl smiled down at her, but he also glanced at Dan. Ivy thought he glared at Dan the way a little boy glared at another little boy who was trying to take away a toy he wasn't done playing with.

"We'll find out who did this to you, baby. I promise we will, and they'll pay."

Ivy pointed to the cup of water on the rolling table by her bed. "Wa … er," she croaked from her scratchy throat. Both men reached for it, but the cup sat nearer to Carl, and he grabbed it first.

"Here you go, baby." He held the straw to Ivy's

dry, cracked lips. She sipped and swallowed slowly. The water flowing down her throat eased the irritation. Carl pulled the straw from her lips. "You better go easy for now."

"Do you need anything else, honey?" Dan asked.

"Cold," Ivy blurted out in a raspy whisper.

Dan pulled the blanket and sheet up over her shoulders and folded it under her chin. "I'll get you a warmed blanket from the nurse's station." Ivy watched him leave the room. Her head becoming less fuzzy, she noted the concern on Dan's face. One of the machines above her head beeped, and Ivy jumped.

This must be terrible for Danny. He's back in a hospital room watching a woman he cares about possibly dying.

Dan returned with a folded blanket and draped it over Ivy. The warmth radiated down over her. It brought back her desire to sleep, and her eyelids fell.

Ivy woke again to see two men in suits standing by her bed. One of them coughed, and Ivy could smell the distinct odor of stale cigarettes. It irritated her, and she sneezed.

"Ms. Chandler," said the heavy man in a blue suit, "I'm Lieutenant Bailey, and this is Sergeant Vincent. We're here to ask you a few questions about what happened to you."

Ivy found the control button to raise her into a sitting position. "I really don't know what I can tell you." Her throat still ached, but she could speak in a raspy voice.

"Did you, by chance, happen to see the person who left the basket on your porch?" Bailey asked.

"The car was leaving by the time I got to the door," Ivy said.

"Did you get a look at the vehicle?" Vincent asked. "Was it a car or a truck?"

"I think it was a truck or maybe an SUV. I only got a quick look, but it sounded bigger than a car."

"Did you see a color?"

"Light color; white or silver maybe," Ivy said and reached for her cup of water. Since waking, Ivy couldn't get enough water. The nurse had told her it was good to drink as much as she could to flush her kidneys of all the toxins left in her system from the toadstools.

"Do you have any idea who might wish you harm, Ms. Chandler?" Bailey asked while taking notes on a little flip pad.

Ivy shook her head. "I can't think of anyone who'd want to hurt me. Cindy Wingate's cousin Peggy who lives down the road isn't too happy about Dan and me living together, but I don't think she'd try to kill me because of it."

"We've spoken with her, and she has an alibi for the time the muffins were dropped off at your house," Vincent said. "Anyhow, her pickup is red."

"How about the men in your life?" Bailey asked without looking up from his notes. "I heard there's been trouble here between Dan Wingate and that other fellow. Anderson, isn't it? What are your relationships with the two of them?"

"Dan and I are living together." Ivy looked up at the detective. "He has an alibi too. He was eating breakfast with me when the person delivered that basket."

"Of course," he said and looked over to the other officer with a raised eyebrow. "And this Anderson fellow? What's your story with him?"

"I've known Carl for a little over a year now. We met in Phoenix."

"And you were having a physical relationship

with him?" Vincent asked with a smug look of disapproval on his face.

I wonder which Bible-thumping church around here he belongs to.

"That ended before I moved here. Carl is otherwise committed to a woman in Phoenix."

"Dan told us there was some animosity between you and this," Bailey flipped through his notepad, "Merriman woman. You and Judith Merriman have had words over this Anderson fellow?"

"No," Ivy said resolutely. "I've only met the woman once in Norman Powell's office. We were introduced by Carl, shook hands, and I left the building with Dan. I haven't seen or spoken to her since."

"And she's never made threats about your relationship with Anderson?" Vincent asked.

"Why would she? Carl and I no longer have a *relationship*."

"According to the staff here, they think Mr. Anderson feels you and he are still an item," Vincent sneered.

"Sergeant," Ivy fumed, "I don't appreciate your tone. Mr. Anderson and I are *not* an *item*. We haven't been since before I moved here. I'm in a very healthy and happy relationship with Dan Wingate."

"Yes," he snorted, "and you're living with the man in the same house he lived in with his late wife. Doesn't that bother the two of you any?"

Ivy turned her head to address Lieutenant Bailey. "I don't see that I have anything more to add to your investigation, and I'm exhausted." Ivy yawned and stretched. "I think I've said all I can."

Bailey flipped his notebook shut, gave Vincent an annoyed glare, and motioned for the other man to leave. "Thank you for your time, Ms. Chandler. We'll be in touch when we have some answers for you."

"Thank you," she said and watched them leave the room.

Good God, I thought people in southern Indiana were tight-laced, but these Missouri folks got them beat by a mile. Are we bothered by living together in Cindy's house? Does he really think we would be living there if it bothered us? What a jerk. I wonder if he *knows where the poison toadstools grow.* Ivy smiled to herself. *Hmm. Catchy title for a book. Who knows where the poison toadstools grow? Maybe I'll use it someday.*

23

The doctor insisted Ivy remain in the hospital for another ten days, saying he wanted to make sure her kidney function continued to do well. Ivy suspected the small rural hospital saw the opportunity for a big payout from her medical insurance carrier and asked the doctor to stall her release for as long as possible.

The vampires from hematology came and drew blood from her arms twice daily. They woke her from a sound sleep at three every morning and came again at three in the afternoon to wake her from her naps. Techs in blue scrubs took her from her room on gurneys for MRI and CT scans. Ivy suffered the terrible food and watched the channel rerunning classic Westerns and sitcoms from the sixties and seventies. She desperately missed her SYFY Channel and Investigation Discovery.

Dan brought her laptop, and Ivy worked on her edits, as well as the third book in her series. She posted on her blog and Facebook page that she was in the hospital with food poisoning and began receiving flowers and cards from people she hardly remembered.

"Isn't this delightful, Danny?" she said one evening, motioning around the room filled with baskets of sweet-smelling arrangements.

"Do you know all these people? Do you have this many close friends and relatives?" Dan asked, sounding dubious.

"Some are relatives, and some are people I knew from high school. I got those two biggest arrangements from my agent and my publisher."

"The agent and publisher I can understand and your sisters and kids," he sighed as he held her hand, "but the rest know you got that big payday for your books and probably hope you'll think kindly of them if they send you flowers." He squeezed her hand tightly. "I bet after you get home, you'll start getting little notes on Facebook, hinting at how they need money for this or that."

"Do you really think so?" Ivy asked sadly.

Dan shrugged his shoulders. "It's usually the way it goes. After Cindy died, you wouldn't believe how many people wanted to know how much of a life insurance payout I got because they were such good friends with Cindy and knew she'd want me to help them out with some of the money."

"Really?" Ivy asked, shocked at the callousness.

"Yes," he said sadly. "I never heard from any of them again after I told them there *was no* life insurance."

"That's too bad." Ivy squeezed his hand but smiled. "Let's collect all the cards, and I'll make a list to see who, and how soon after I get home, starts contacting me with requests for help with their problems. How's Cheshire doing?"

"He misses you," Dan told her. "He lays out on the swing waiting for ya and yowls at night if I don't bring the damned cushion in for him to sleep on, and it has to be exactly in front of the fireplace, or he has fits." Dan laughed.

"Thanks for looking after him, Danny. I really appreciate it." Ivy moved around in the bed to ease the strain on her backside from being in bed too long. She got up and walked the halls regularly because the nurses told her she needed to keep her muscles from tightening up and for her circulation.

"It's no problem, sweetheart. I've been working on the carport and the deck, and Cheshire doesn't like the hammering or the sound of the saw one little bit." He laughed. "Have those cops been back around?" Danny asked.

Ivy shook her head. "I haven't heard another word from them. After talking to them, I really doubt they give a shit who tried to kill us." She saw Dan's eyes widen. "Whoever it was knew you were there with me. They probably thought we'd both eat the damned things." Ivy paused. "And what if I'd given some to Cheshire? He's a little guy, and it probably wouldn't have taken much to kill him." She shivered at the thought. "Have you seen Carl around? He hasn't been here in days."

"Maybe he finally got the damned idea that you didn't want him around anymore and went home." Dan yawned and stretched.

"Why don't you go on home? You've been working hard and must be worn out." Ivy patted his hand.

"Yeah, I think I will. I need to bring Cheshire's cushion in," he laughed, "he's probably throwing a fit about now." Dan bent and kissed Ivy deeply. "I'll be glad when you get home," he whispered.

"You and me too." She sighed and pulled him close for one last kiss before he left. "I love you."

"Me too."

Ivy's eyes followed Dan's handsome behind out the door and into the hall. Once she lost sight of him, Ivy turned her attention back to the television and finished watching a replaying of Truman Capote's *In Cold Blood.* She drifted off to sleep before Robert Blake swung from the gallows.

Ivy woke to someone clearing his throat. Half asleep, she assumed it would be one of the vampires coming to draw blood. The sight of Carl standing illuminated only by the monitor next to by her bed startled Ivy fully awake.

"Carl, what are you doing here so late?" Ivy asked as she roused herself into a sitting position. It surprised her to realize the room was in total darkness except for the blue glow of the buzzing television, no longer offering programming at the late hour. She saw no light from the hall with the door to her room closed.

"I came to say goodbye," he said softly.

"Are you leaving then?" Ivy asked, yawning.

"No," he whispered, "you are."

"What?" Ivy asked in confusion. She had no plans to travel.

"You've ruined me, Ivy Chandler," Carl growled. He had a hard look in his eyes Ivy had never seen before, and it frightened her.

"What are you talking about, Carl?" Ivy asked, beginning to feel a bit of desperation. She moved her hand toward the call button for the nurse's station. Thankfully, it lay concealed under the blankets beside her leg.

"Because of you," Carl accused, "Judith has pulled her funding from all my projects and is calling in all her loans to me. I'm ruined, and it's all because of a low-rent piece of ass I couldn't keep my cock out of."

"Carl, what the hell are you talking about? I haven't done anything to you." Ivy's hand finally found the call device, and her finger desperately searched for the appropriate button.

"Judith thought I intended to propose to her on that trip, and when she saw you here, she thought I'd made arrangements to meet you behind her back. She got all worked up on the flight back to Phoenix, and when she got home, she began the process of dissolving our business relationship. She and her bunch of vulture lawyers are snatching up all the properties we bought together.

"You've ruined me, baby. You lured me in with that tight little hillbilly snatch of yours and kept in touch just enough so I couldn't get your filthy tight asshole off my mind." Carl jerked a pillow from beneath her head. Ivy began pressing the buttons on the call device. The television flicked off, casting the room into near full darkness.

Carl pressed the pillow into her face, cutting off her oxygen. Ivy struggled but continued to press the buttons on the device she hoped called for assistance from the nurse's station.

"I paid one of these stupid hillbillies to bake you those special muffins and drop them off, but she screwed that up, and that damned truck driver never left your side long enough for me to do this while you were out cold. I waited in the lobby tonight until I saw him go. You've ruined me, baby. And I promised myself I'd *end* you tonight."

Ivy saw her grandpa sitting on the porch, and Granny stood by the open front door. They noticed her but didn't beckon to her to come forward. They stood together, serenely smiling, and waited for her to move toward them. Ivy wanted to take a step forward out of the cool shade of the big maple, but something held her back. A voice from behind called out her name. Ivy turned back, sadly, to her waiting grandparents. They both smiled and waved as if telling her to turn away once more. They called her to tell her they'd be there waiting when it *was* time.

Ivy opened her eyes to blinding lights above her bed. Someone pounded on her chest, forcing air into her lungs. Ivy jerked up, gasping for breath. Someone grabbed her and pulled her back down onto the bed. He slipped an oxygen mask over her mouth and nose. Ivy gulped in the oxygen that helped to clear her head. Her eyes darted around, looking for Carl.

Oh, my God. It was Carl. Carl tried to kill me. He tried to kill me twice. Oh, my God.

The sadness of the realization overwhelmed Ivy, and she felt herself drifting into unconsciousness once more. She wanted to sleep. If she slept, it would all just go away. Ivy wanted to sleep.

The warm morning sun shone onto her face from the window the next time Ivy opened her eyes. She sensed someone beside her bed. Remembering Carl's vicious attack, Ivy snatched herself away.

"It's OK, honey. It's Dan."

Ivy calmed, recognizing his voice. "Danny," Ivy wept, "it was Carl. Carl tried to kill me." She spoke as though she had a cold with a stuffy nose.

"I know," his voice soothed. "The nurse called me. I came right away, but you were sleeping. Are you alright?"

Ivy raised a hand to her throbbing nose. She felt a bandage and something metal.

"They said he broke your nose when he tried to smother you. Don't *even* ask me for a mirror," Dan said, rolling his eyes and trying to sound light-hearted.

"Why?" Ivy asked and touched her tender face again.

Smiling, Dan took out his cell phone and snapped a picture. Ivy watched him grin before he handed her the four-inch phone. On the screen, Ivy looked back with a bandage in the center of her face, held in place by a delicate metal brace, between two swollen purple bulges with narrow weeping slits where her eyes should be.

"Oh, my God," she mumbled, and rage at Carl surged through her. "Where is the fucking son-of-a-bitch?"

"He's gone, Ivy," Dan said softly, taking her hand.

"What do you mean he's gone? Did they let him get out of the hospital? Are the police looking for him?" Ivy demanded.

"The hospital security guys stopped him, and the police took him away," Dan told her. "But on the way to the jail, he had a massive heart attack, and by the time they got him back here to the hospital, Carl was gone."

"Oh," was all Ivy could say as a sense of relief flooded over her. She closed her eyes and drifted back into sleep, wondering who waited for Carl on the other side.

Dan was there at her side when she woke again, and they shared a dinner of instant mashed potatoes, soggy chicken nuggets, mushy green peas, warm peach slices, and weak sweet tea. Ivy hated tea, and Dan went to the vending machine and got her a root beer.

"This food sucks," Dan said with a grimace. "When you get home, I'm gonna cook you a meal of real fried chicken and mashed potatoes."

"That sounds awesome," Ivy sighed. "I actually dream about eating real food in this place."

"I can imagine. The doc told me you could probably go home in a day or two. I guess the police asked them to keep you in here just in case someone tried to hurt you again."

Rage suddenly surged through Ivy. "You mean those fat bastards were using me like bait in here?"

"No, they thought you'd be safer here than at the house."

"Well, they certainly fucked up there. Didn't they?" Ivy shook her head, and a frustrated tear ran down her cheek. Carl had tried to kill her twice, and now he lay dead on a cold slab in a coroner's office somewhere. He'd been her lover. She'd even thought she'd loved him. How could things have gone so very wrong?

24

Dan picked her up at the hospital three days after Carl's attack and death. His children had collected his body and taken him back to Wisconsin for burial. Someone had left a *USA Today* on her tray table folded to a page featuring Carl's photo from the Tulsa tornado coverage. The headline said something about 'From Hero to Attempted Murderer.' Ivy refused to read it and tossed it into the trash can beside her bed.

The doctor had removed the bandage from her nose, and Ivy was happy to see it had no deformity. The swelling under her eyes had subsided, but there would be dark circles beneath them for several weeks to come, the doctor assured her.

A blue-smocked young man wheeled her down to the front door, where Dan met her with the Lexus. Ivy had never been so happy as the minute they wheeled her out into the fresh air and sunshine. She never wanted to step inside a hospital again.

Ivy slid into the car and strapped on her seatbelt. Dan tossed the plastic bag of hospital sundries into the back seat.

"Can I tempt you with a little pulled pork and slaw?" Dan asked.

"Oh, God, yes," Ivy nearly begged.

They drove up to the BBQ joint, and Dan went inside. Ivy remained in the car and did her best to hide her face when people looked her way. Her hair looked a mess, and her face would probably frighten small children.

Dan returned with a large brown paper bag and two large Styrofoam cups with lids. Ivy took the cups while Dan stowed the bag on the floor near her feet. The aroma of smoked pork filled the Lexus, and Ivy's mouth watered with anticipation.

When they drove into the drive, Ivy very nearly didn't recognize the place. She couldn't believe it had very nearly been a month since they'd driven out of the drive for the lumber yard that day.

"Oh, my God, Danny," Ivy gasped, taking in the new addition to her country home. She stepped out of the car into a two-car carport, built from lumber stained to match the cabin. "I can't believe this."

Dan walked around the front of the car and opened the door for Ivy, who still held the cups of soda. Dan picked up the bag of food. "Come this way, my love." He put a strong arm around her shoulders and walked with her to a set of three steps with a railing, leading up onto the new deck.

Ivy marveled at the additions. To her left, the deck led to a short step up, connecting the new deck to the front porch. Posts and lattices made a secluding fence of sorts around the new deck area. "This is beautiful, Danny." Terracotta pots of blooming marigolds, petunias, and mums rested atop each post.

"You ain't seen nothin' yet, woman." Dan turned her around and walked her to the other end of the new deck. An enclosure with a roof had been added from the edge of the back door about fifteen feet to the end of the existing cabin. Dan opened glass-paned French doors and ushered Ivy into a tropical paradise. The floor, covered with green indoor-outdoor carpet, held a bubbling, octagonal tub dropped into the center of the room. "No climbing over tall sides to get in," Dan chuckled, "you can just step right in."

"Oh, my God, Danny," Ivy said as tears of joy ran down her bruised face. Around the tub, he'd arranged the wicker patio furniture. The bright red cushions stood out against the bright green carpet on the floor, and Ivy thought it looked beautiful. A tall potted tree stood in one corner, and pots of pink and orangey-red begonias hung in front of walls made from tall glass panels. Ivy looked up to see two glass panels set into the ceiling as well. "This is beautiful, Danny," she wept, "just beautiful."

"Well, when it gets cold, you're not gonna be able to sit out on that swing and write your stories, so I thought this would be a good alternative." He hugged her and kissed the top of her head. "Do you like it?" he asked hesitantly.

"Like it?" Ivy exclaimed. "I love it." She wrapped her arms around Dan and kissed him on the mouth, careful of her still painful nose. "Now, I have my country cabin and my Victorian solarium." She spun around the bright, sun-filled room, smiling. "I'm gonna have to see if Humphry has any wrought-iron accent pieces in his store like a big birdcage for one of the corners and some hooks for the towels."

"Oh, good lord," Dan sighed, taking Ivy's thin, ravaged body into his strong, protective arms once more, "and it begins again."

Dear reader,

We hope you enjoyed reading *Promises*. Please take a moment to leave a review, even if it's a short one. Your opinion is important to us.

Discover more books by Lori Beasley Bradley at
https://www.nextchapter.pub/authors/lori-beasley-bradley

Want to know when one of our books is free or discounted? Join the newsletter at
http://eepurl.com/bqqB3H

Best regards,
Lori Beasley Bradley and the Next Chapter Team

ACKNOWLEDGMENTS

This book is dedicated to Adam Sterling, my friend, my mentor, my booster, and my muse. Thanks for all your support and encouragement. You always make it into my books. Sorry, I kill you so often, but you see a lot of action. I hope you enjoy living--and dying vicariously on my pages.

Promises
ISBN: 978-4-86750-238-9
Mass Market

Published by
Next Chapter
1-60-20 Minami-Otsuka
170-0005 Toshima-Ku, Tokyo
+818035793528

4th June 2021